SYL VAN DUYN

Syl van Duyn has published several Dutch language children's books: *Hallo Aarde, Hier Maan* (2001), *Mijn Zus is een Flussemus* (2002), *Angels* (2008) and *Op zoek naar jou* (2015), as well as an adult non-fiction book based on the columns she wrote for the Dutch magazine, *Margriet*, titled *Een kwetsbaar bestaan* (2001). She works for the Dutch broadcasting network VPRO, selecting and purchasing documentaries, and lives in Amsterdam.

ERNESTINE HOEGEN

Ernestine Hoegen worked as a public prosecutor before turning to writing, translating and editing full-time in 2017. Her biography of Dutchwoman Mieke Bouman, *Een strijdbaar bestaan. Mieke Bouman en de Indonesische strafprocessen* (Spectrum, Amsterdam) has recently been published. She lives near Arnhem.

First published in the UK in 2020 by Aurora Metro Publications Ltd.

67 Grove Avenue, Twickenham, TW1 4HX

www.aurorametro.com info@aurorametro.com

T: @aurorametro FB/AuroraMetroBooks

Girl Out Of Place (Searching for you) © Syl van Duyn 2020

English translation of *Girl Out Of Place (Searching for You)* © Ernestine Hoegen 2020

Cover images: Shutterstock

Cover design: © 2020 Aurora Metro Publications Ltd.

Editor: Cheryl Robson

Aurora Metro Books would like to thank Marina Tuffier, Zainab Raghdo and Lianna Tosetti

All rights are strictly reserved. For rights enquiries please contact the publisher: info@aurorametro.com

No part of this publication may be reproduced, stored in or introduced into a retrieval system, or transmitted in any form, or by any means (electronic, mechanical, photocopying, recording or otherwise) without the prior permission of the publisher. Any person who does any unauthorised act in relation to this publication may be liable to criminal prosecution and civil claims for damages.

This paperback is sold subject to the condition that it shall not, by way of trade or otherwise, be lent, resold, hired out, or otherwise circulated without the publisher's prior consent in any form of binding or cover other than that in which it is published and without a similar condition being imposed on the subsequent purchaser.

Printed by 4edge Printers, Essex, UK on FSC grade paper.

ISBNs: 978-1-912430-43-7 (print)/978-1-912430-44-4 (ebook)

This publication has been made possible with financial support from the Dutch Foundation for Literature.

GIRL OUT OF PLACE

BY

SYL VAN DUYN

Translated by Ernestine Hoegen

AURORA METRO BOOKS

For Nora

CONTENTS

Getting Away	9
The Long Journey	19
Jogjakarta	22
Looking For My Father	33
Living In A Proper House Again	37
News Of My Father	49
Merdeka	53
Bersiap: Be Prepared	62
We Have To Get Away From Here	71
Waiting	81
To Singapore	93
Where Is Everyone?	105
Here I Am	110
Don't Make Me Do Things	118
Jakarta Is Not For Girls	121
Bondi: The Place To Be	131
Surprise	140
Carefree Days	150
Too Bad	166
To Sydney	181
The Garden Of Eden	185
What Use Is A Father Like That?	191
Where's The Sun?	206
I'm Here For You	214
A New Destination	222
Glossary	228
Author's Endnote	229

My mother has forgotten my name
My child does not yet know what I'm called.
How do I know I'm safe?
Name me, confirm my existence,
Let my name be like a chain.
Call me, call me, talk to me,
Oh, call me by my deepest name.
For those I love, I need a name.

Maria Min

GETTING AWAY

I was fifteen and I had never kissed a boy. Of course, there were no boys of my age to kiss, because I was living in a dreadful internment camp, deep in the jungle, somewhere in the mountains beyond Semarang. We were prisoners of the Japanese army, which had occupied the island of Java a few years before, forcing many of us Westerners into detention camps, like this one at Ambarawa. It's not a place I like to think about, now, as life there was harsh and sometimes cruel. We all prayed for the war to be over, so we could go back home to our house in Jogjakarta. But then, not long after the Japs surrendered, the day came when my aunt told me quietly, 'Nell, we're leaving, tomorrow. Make sure you pack everything and you're ready to go.'

You'd think I would have been excited and had all my stuff packed in a flash. But no, I really didn't want to go. You see, I couldn't abandon my mother, who lay all alone in a bamboo coffin under the ground. She had been buried in the open field beside the yard, where we used to stand in rows for hours every morning to bow to the Japs. She'd been dead for three months by then. But still, I found it hard to leave.

Aunt Karly explained to me that the allies had dropped bombs on Hiroshima and Nagasaki, in Japan, which had ended the war. But the Japs were still there in the camp because they had to protect us from the Indonesian people, who wanted their independence from the Dutch. I hated politics. And all the strife. It only led to war. And you lost the people you loved the most.

'Now that we can go, we're leaving no matter what happens,' said Aunt Karly, firmly.

That's why I'd woken up really early that morning. The sun had just risen and was beginning to warm the field. The dreary camp was quiet. Most people still lay under their mosquito nets, but I'd gone outside in my underwear.

The building used to be a Catholic school, and this was one of the classrooms. I was standing in the doorway of classroom 4G. The Japs had very cleverly arranged wooden bunks along the walls and even right in the middle of the room. That way, they could cram as many people as possible into one room. I had a small mattress on the bunk along the left side where I slept under a mosquito net beside my aunt. Our few belongings were stowed beneath our bunk. There were even more people crammed onto the bunk next to us.

Alert to all the sounds, I leaned against the outer wall of the classroom. All I could see was the steeple of the school chapel and the peaks of the surrounding mountains. Some days, the clouds completely covered them. The barbed wire fence and the guards in their watch towers usually meant that everyone stayed in their rooms. Today I wanted to absorb everything. I wanted to be able to tell people what this place was really like, and I didn't want to forget a single thing. I listened to the silence. The mountains, the camp buildings and the watch towers still had to shake off the lingering darkness and resume their usual place in the world. Ever since the day my mother had ceased to be there beside me in the tiny bed in classroom 4G, ever since she had been taken away to be laid in the field, I often got up before dawn.

Because I was leaving, I wanted to remember every detail of this place. How the first ray of sunlight tinged the morning sky with shades of purple while the same light made the mountains glow white. It was that time of the day when everything seemed possible and the violet light softened everything. It was as if my mother was still here, as if she could touch me and I could feel her. We were very similar, my mother and me. We both tended to be impatient – and to be honest, I was much more impatient than my mother. We had the same slender build, the same unruly mass of brownish curls, the same amber-coloured eyes, the same crease between our eyebrows that appeared when we were worrying about something.

Could I really leave this place? For years, I'd prayed to be able to go. Away from the dirt and the unbearable stench, away from the single cold water tap in the camp, which usually wasn't working. I was always thirsty. I was always hungry. There was never enough food. Yes, of course Aunt Karly and I had to get out of here. Now that the war was over, I wanted to look for my father. I needed to know where he was. I wanted to feel his arms around me. I wanted to hear his voice again, gently teasing me 'And how is my little Nelly today?' I wanted to go back to the time when everything was safe, and we were all still living together. That was three years ago, three years since I'd seen him. I had to hurry, pack my few things, and get out. *Mustn't waste any time!* I went inside and took my things out from under the mosquito net. Of course, my father didn't know the worst thing of all — that on 26th April we'd carried my mother out of the camp to lay her in the field beyond and that I was now alone with my aunt. *Mustn't think about that now.* It would only make me cry and I didn't want to cry anymore. I had to get ready to leave.

I laid our little saucepan and our two cups out on a piece of batik cloth. On top of that I laid my threadbare and now, much too short, blue skirt together with a white vest. Then I rolled up my mosquito net and placed it on top of the other things. Lastly, I put my mother's smart woollen coat on top of the pile, and I tried to tie the corners of the cloth into a bundle. Why was I having so much trouble? I was trying to do it too fast, of course. I had to put everything together again neatly and pull really hard on the corners of the cloth to be able to tie them together. 'A beautiful *bungkusan*,' my mother would have said. *Mustn't think about it.* I pulled on my green skirt and white blouse, slipped on my worn sandals, and walked out of the room.

Outside, at the corner of the yard, a young Jap was standing guard. It was the same young man who, three months ago, had walked with my aunt and me behind the bamboo coffin. An Indonesian had pushed the coffin on a cart over to the field. There, the coffin had disappeared into a shallow hole. My eyes searched once more for the right spot in the grassy field. I had no choice but how could I leave my mother behind over there? All alone.

Why was everything so complicated? Staying here or going. The young Jap soldier stood there exactly as he had always stood there, but he wasn't looking as severe as before. Just now, I hadn't bowed for him and I hadn't been punished. He hadn't beaten me, but had just ignored me, pretended he hadn't seen me. Although his emperor had capitulated a week ago, he couldn't get away from here either. He had no choice but to stay where he was.

Aunt Karly came to stand next to me. The dress she was wearing with the frayed white collar was much too big for her, but she still looked pretty. The faded blue dress matched the colour of her eyes. She wore her hair in a plait down her back and for the first time I noticed that she'd gone almost entirely grey. When had that happened? She put an arm around me, and we stood like that for a moment, as if frozen in time. Then my aunt pulled away.

'You know, you really are allowed to leave.'

I didn't react.

'I'm certain your mother would want us to get away from Ambarawa.'

'How do you know that?' I mumbled.

'Because I know Elenore really well. We have to leave here now that we have the chance. Believe me, going to Surabaya is the best option.'

I was silent. Tears burned behind my eyes, but I willed them away. It was true. I couldn't stay. I had to get away from here. My aunt always knew what was right. She never doubted herself, or worried about the risk — she just did what she felt was necessary.

I went inside and tried to muster my courage. I looked at the mosquito nets, the mattresses, the shabby things stored under the bunks. I listened to the sounds of the children playing outside. I registered all those ordinary goings on and pulled myself together.

'Alright. Let's get out of here,' I said, with a croaky voice. It sounded braver than I felt.

'But I can't leave without saying goodbye to Lisa, first.' My friend, Lisa, with her deep blue eyes, black plaits and gangly body. We'd worked together in the camp kitchen and I was really fond of her. I'd had a lot of laughs with Lisa de Vries. She was an only child, too, and her father had died when she was little. Her mother had never remarried. I couldn't leave without saying goodbye.

'I'll be right back,' I said, and ran off.

Saying you are leaving is not the same thing as actually leaving! I stood with my aunt in the yard and felt sick. I hadn't been able to find Lisa anywhere. 'Please, can't we wait just a little longer?' I asked. 'Perhaps she'll turn up somewhere.'

'No, we really have to go now,' she said. 'We're already late.'

I sighed. 'So, can we just walk out of the gate now? Why didn't we do that before?'

'You know that wasn't possible before. You would have been killed immediately. They would have beaten us to death,' she said with a determined look on her face. 'Now that it turns out that their emperor is not as invincible as they thought he was, things have changed. They won't stop us. Not if they're sensible. They'd rather make themselves invisible and keep quiet.'

I grabbed hold of her hand. 'Thank goodness you're older and braver than I am. And you know what to do.'

Aunt Karly laughed. 'That remains to be seen, but I'm doing my best. The first thing is to walk out of this camp without being arrested. Come on, let's go.'

Together we walked to the gate. I held on to my little bundle tightly with one hand and clutched Aunt Karly's arm with the other. The watchtowers were placed in such a way that no one could leave the camp unseen. The guards must have been watching us all along, but they didn't show it. They didn't react, didn't protest, didn't try to stop us. I looked at Aunt Karly. She nodded at me. 'Keep walking.'

She looked very determined. I thought she knew what she was doing, but I sensed her nervousness in her footsteps as we passed through the gate to the other side of the *gedek*, the bamboo fencing around the camp. My heart was beating twice as fast as normal and I felt the blood pounding in my temples. Sweat trickled down my back. When we were finally on the other side of the gate my aunt stopped and loosened my grip on her arm. My fingers had left white marks.

'Well done, Nell,' she said, encouragingly.

I wanted to look back at the open field where my mother lay, but I didn't dare to. I put my bundle down and rubbed my aunt's arm.

'I'm sorry I squeezed you so hard. I was so scared that we would be arrested, but there isn't a single Jap who took any notice!' I looked at the people from the camp who had gathered by the *gedek*. Even at this early hour, people were busy bargaining with people from outside the camp, trading their meagre belongings for food.

'Look at that!' I cried, excitedly. 'Two eggs for a worn shirt. A cup of rice for an old pair of shorts.' Normally the Japs punished bartering harshly, but now they looked away and didn't bother.

'We have to keep going,' said Aunt Karly. 'Come on! Keep walking! We're the first to leave the camp today. We have to get to Ambarawa station early. I want to catch the train as soon as possible.'

I picked up my bundle and hurried on. I felt the eyes of the guards boring into my back and I wanted to turn around, but I didn't dare to, in case they came after us.

'Don't worry about them,' said Aunt Karly. She clenched her hands into fists. 'They're not going to drag us back into the camp and they're not going to leave us standing in the middle of that sweltering hot yard tied to a post all day as punishment anymore. They're not going to leave us doubled up in a crate for a few days anymore either. Now that they've been beaten, they're not allowed to do that. Although, of course, you can never be sure with those Japs. Just keep up with me, Nell, and don't stop.'

I did as she asked. I tried not to look back and to think of other things. But it was difficult, because my whole being was screaming that I had to look back one last time at the grassy field where my mother lay. So as not to think about that, I changed the subject: 'It looks different to when we arrived here.'

'There's only one road from the station to the Ambarawa camp. Three years ago, it was almost dark and a lot cooler when we arrived.'

'Yes, it's sweltering now. Back then, I thought that the war would be over soon and that I'd be home in a few weeks. I didn't know any better.'

'We all thought that.'

I sighed. I was terribly hot and was finding it increasingly difficult to keep on walking and to keep up with my aunt's pace. The sun was right overhead, and the sweat was running down my back. My bundle felt even heavier. I moved it to my other hand. On our way here, a long time ago now, my mother had carried most of our belongings. My mother... *Mustn't think about her. Mustn't look round to try and catch a last glimpse of the little field where she lay, abandoned.*

I thought of Orpheus. My father liked telling me that story. He told me that he loved my mother just as much as Orpheus loved his wife Eurydice. 'Do you know the story about Orpheus, Auntie? It was mine and Dad's favourite.'

'Do tell!' she said, sensing that I was looking for distraction and glad that we could talk about something else.

'Orpheus was inconsolable when his beloved bride, Eurydice, died on the day of their wedding, and he cried so much that eventually his tears softened the hearts of the gods. He was allowed to bring her back from the underworld on condition that he would come all the way back to the upper world without once glancing back at Eurydice, who was walking behind him out of Hades.'

'But Orpheus looked back, didn't he?'

'Yes, he ruined everything by looking round and then his beloved bride was gone. Disappeared forever.'

'But you can look back at your mother's grave, you know.'

I looked at my aunt, angrily. 'I do know that my mother is not going to come back to life whether I look back there or not. I know perfectly well that people don't rise from the dead. Not Eurydice, and not my mother, but if I look around, the Japs might see me and take me back.'

It was not until these last words came out that I realized that I was shouting. I threw my bundle down into the road. Two birds with blue feathers flapped out of a coconut palm. I watched them go as the tears ran down my face. Two little heads with a white spot and a black circle around the eyes, a red bill and little red legs: paddy birds. My mother would have called them *glatiks*. She never wanted me to use the Dutch names for native birds.

'Let's swap over, you're carrying too much.' Aunt Karly took off her rucksack and put it down next to my bundle. I wanted to object, to say that I wanted to carry my own stuff, but before I could say anything, she had already picked up my *bungkusan*.

'What have you got in there?'

I didn't answer but watched as my aunt pulled my bundle apart. 'No wonder this is so heavy. Why did you bring along that woollen coat?'

I didn't say anything, not even that that was a stupid question. My mother had lugged that coat all the way to Ambarawa. My father had given her that coat as a gift in

America and now it had to be taken back to him. Auntie smoothed the coat with both hands. Her hands were trembling. She bent over, put her face into the soft woollen material, just like I often did, but without anyone noticing. Then Aunt Karly pulled herself upright. 'Silly of me. Of course, that coat has to come with us.' I saw that there were tears in her eyes. 'Goodbye Elenore, goodbye my dear friend,' she whispered, so softly that it was barely audible. Then she tied up the bundle, tighter than necessary. 'Let's go.'

I picked up the rucksack and as I slung it over my shoulder, a sudden urge made me look back. Ambarawa already lay far behind us. In the distance, the top of the small white church steeple was just visible, and my mother had disappeared forever.

THE LONG JOURNEY

'You can't be serious. Three more hours?' I looked up at Aunt Karly in disbelief. I was sat leaning against the cool wall of the station building in the shade of the portico. It wasn't busy. A few Indonesians were selling food, and there were about ten other people from the camp who I didn't really know, who were sitting just as I was with their luggage on the platform. Aunt Karly had just come back from getting the tickets.

'Why so long?' Tears of disappointment stung behind my eyes. The journey from the camp to the station had seemed endless but I knew that I mustn't give up. Every step took me closer to the station, closer to freedom. It was only now that I was sitting here, that I felt how tired I was. My cotton blouse stuck to my back, my skirt itched, and my sandals were dusty from the red sand of the road. A feeling of exhaustion came over me.

'That's ages away. I want to take a nap on the train.'

Aunt Karly came over and sat next to me on the ground. 'Just think of it like we've been waiting for this train for over three years. Who cares about three more hours, just as long as we can get away?'

I shrugged my shoulders. She was right, but I didn't want to admit that, so I asked about the tickets. 'Did you have enough money?'

'Enough to get us from here to Surabaya.' She pulled out two tickets and waved them about. I immediately saw that her ring was missing, the silver ring inlaid with purple amethyst. For as long as I could remember, my aunt had worn that ring. It was in the camp that I had first noticed how, in the evenings, her light blue eyes were set off by the purplish colour of the stone. Every now and then, I had begged her to let me wear the ring, but she refused. 'That ring is precious to me! Your parents gave it to me, and I certainly don't want to lose it. They brought that ring back with them from their trip to America. According to the Indians, amethyst ensures restorative sleep, sleep without nightmares. I'm afraid that, without that ring, I won't be able to sleep.'

'Why didn't they give me a ring like that?'

'You won the lottery, you went to America with them,' answered Aunt Karly, and however much I whined, I was never allowed to try the ring. And now it was gone. Traded for two single train rides to Surabaya. I felt embarrassed, ashamed of myself. 'Just grow up, Nelly Arends,' my father would have said. From now on, I wouldn't complain about anything. I gave my aunt a hug. 'Is there anything I can do?'

'Sing me a lullaby tonight,' she said with a laugh, but her eyes weren't laughing. She stood up and pointed to a black steam engine and three green railway carriages that were sitting in a siding further down the railway tracks.

'That's our train to Jogjakarta. We change there. Our train leaves in three hours. We'll be alright.'

I went over to stand next to her. 'The middle carriage – third class?' My stomach rumbled. I was hungry, but I didn't want to moan about that now.

'The middle carriage, but first let's see if that *pisang* vendor will sell us something. I still have a little money,' said Aunt Karly, as if she had read my thoughts.

JOGJAKARTA

I was woken up by the shrill sound of the whistle of the steam engine. I heard the train draw into the station and come to a wheezing, grinding halt in Jogjakarta. When I looked out, I saw it was almost night-time. The mountains were dark against the red evening sky. The train journey on the narrow wooden benches hadn't been as bad as I had expected.

'Sleep well?' asked Aunt Karly.

I nodded and stretched. 'I was hoping to look out of the window for the whole trip.'

'It's always hot on the train. That makes you drop off easily. Stay close by me when we get off, alright? I don't want to lose you in the crowds at the station.'

'I promise, I'll stay close by. What would I do without you in Jogjakarta?' I laughed. I ran to the door and was the first to jump off the train onto the platform. It was crowded. There were a lot more trains here than in Ambarawa. The station was a big white colonial building with a grand concourse and many tall windows, high wooden doors, and beautiful high ceilings. Because of the white plastered walls, it was cool. In between the throng of Indonesians, I could see people from the camp sitting around with all sorts of luggage. Wooden boxes, suitcases, rucksacks, woven baskets in all shapes and sizes, rolled up mats, bundles of clothes, mattresses and some people had even managed to bring live chickens. Most of them seemed to have made a small camp on the platform, as if they didn't expect to be going anywhere soon. But I wasn't going to stay here that long.

Aunt Karly caught up with me and crossly grabbed hold of my arm. 'Don't say one thing and do another, do you hear me!'

'Sorry,' I said, shaken. 'I just couldn't help myself. There's so much to see here, but you're right. I won't do it again.'

'You'd better not. I know you're keen to see everything, but we really must stay together!'

I nodded and guiltily walked behind my aunt to the west side of the station, where it wasn't so crowded. There, we looked for a spot to wait for the next train. We threw my bundle and the rucksack on the ground, and with her last coins Aunt Karly bought some *nasi* and tea from one of the vendors, passing by with foodstuffs. We sat next to our luggage with our backs against the wall, contentedly.

'Now there's food, you come and sit right beside me.' Auntie winked at me and gave me a portion of *nasi*.

I tried to eat slowly, but I was so hungry that I couldn't. In two or three greedy mouthfuls, I had finished my bit of food, and downed the tea straight after. 'Delicious!'

I felt Aunt Karly looking at me, but she didn't say anything and ate her rice with tiny little nibbles.

In the twilight, shafts of light fell through the tall windows. It made the metal of the railway tracks shine, and the dust particles caught in the light, were glowing golden above the station building. It felt surreal to be sitting there so quietly with my aunt in the big station before nightfall. It seemed an eternity ago that we had walked out of the camp. For the first time since our departure, I didn't feel as if I had to take orders anymore. I wanted to hold my aunt's hand and at the same moment she felt for my hand. Our fingers collided, entwined and we sat like that for a while without saying anything.

The midnight train to Surabaya consisted of a steam engine and three carriages. I had been standing for about an hour with Aunt Karly at the front of the queue, waiting to board. We didn't say much. I suddenly remembered that I had been here with my mother before the war started. Would Aunt Karly know that?

'I made this trip with my mother, too. That time when we went from Jogjakarta to visit Granny and you in Surabaya.'

'I remember,' said Aunt Karly. 'February '42. The Japs had just landed on Sumatra and could reach Java at any moment. You couldn't stay on your own in the house in Jogja.'

'Yes, my father took me and my mother to the station. He kissed us both and said: "We'll see each other again soon at Granny's." There was no time for him to wave us off, he had to drive straight to the airfield of Tasikmalaya. He rushed off as if he didn't have a moment to lose, because the war was coming.'

'I always thought my brother looked very handsome in his Royal Dutch East Indies uniform.'

I shrugged. I didn't agree with my aunt at all, but I didn't say so. Wearing that uniform and his captain's cap, my father didn't seem like my father at all, and the day that he left for war in his uniform, was also the last time I saw him. I shook back my curls. *Stop thinking those thoughts.* I looked at the pushing throng behind us, laden with big packs, and listened to the buzzing voices of people in the station. I went to stand closer to my aunt.

'I've never seen so many people together before. I never knew that people could make so much noise and I don't believe that all those people will fit into the train.'

'Stay close by me,' said Aunt Karly, sternly, 'then nothing will happen.'

'Of course, I'll stay near you.' I couldn't bear to think of losing her. Without her, I was bound to be trampled under the feet of the crowd. I held on to a strap of her rucksack. With my other hand, I clenched my bundle so tightly that the knuckles of my fingers turned white.

'That three-hour wait this morning at Ambarawa was nothing compared to this,' she said.

'I'd rather be standing in line in the camp waiting for my food!' I grumbled.

Aunt Karly turned around and glared at me and the strap I was holding, flew out of my grasp.

'Sorry, that's not true. I never want to go back to the camp.'

She turned back and before I could get hold of the strap of her rucksack again, the crowd started moving. Suddenly, I was being pushed and pulled from all sides as I was shoved forward by the crowd. Then I noticed that my aunt was already on the train and was calling out to me.

'Wait, wait!' I screamed, 'Don't leave me!' I threw my body forward and held my bundle high above the mass of people. A rippling movement of the crowd on the platform brought me to the front of the train. I was in a complete panic and I shouted: 'Wait! I've got to get on too! Aunt Karly! Don't leave me!'

I could hardly breathe. It felt as if there were ten sacks of sand pushing against my chest, but I couldn't give up. I had to go with her. Just as I was about to be squashed by the pressing crowd, someone on the balcony of the train grabbed hold of my arms.

'Hold on!' shouted a young man's voice. Two hands pulled me through the sea of people and over the iron railing until I was hauled up onto the balcony. Somebody else threw my *bungkusan* after me onto the train. The cries of angry people on the platform swelled as the train slowly set itself in motion. I lay stretched out on the balcony with my eyes closed. After a while, I could breathe normally again. I was lying on the floor of the train to Surabaya and Aunt Karly was on the same train. I had kept my promise, I had stayed with her. I hadn't lost her. Well, almost.

When I opened my eyes, I saw a square boyish face, with long dark unruly hair. Hazel eyes with white flecks looked at me searchingly for a moment. I could only look back. For a second, we floated together through space until, confused, I was the first to look away.

'Are you alright?'

'I think so.' I got a better look at my rescuer. He had a small nose with lots of freckles, and a mouth with full lips. Lips, that curled up at the corners, ready to laugh. It was a mouth, that I would have liked to kiss. Why on earth did I think that? I felt my face turning red.

'Good!' He pulled me to my feet. I saw immediately that we were about the same height. Two thin legs protruded from his khaki shorts.

'My name is Tim. Tim Thissen. Do you always board a train like that?' He looked at me, questioningly. The intense look in his eyes had gone, but he was still a very nice-looking young man. So nice-looking that his touch made the hairs on my arms stand up.

'I'm Nelly Arends,' I said, and then the absurdity of our introduction struck me. From sheer nerves, I started laughing really loudly. I couldn't stop even though it hurt my whole body, which was bruised from landing on the balcony of the train. 'I don't usually get on like that,' I said, when I could talk again. Meanwhile, my aunt had made her way up the train and threw her arms around me. 'Are you alright, Nell?'

I nodded and she rattled on. 'Thank goodness you're on the train! You made it onboard and you can still laugh about it! I'm so glad!' She held me for a moment and teasingly ruffled my hair.

I felt her concern in her touch, heard the joy in her voice. For the first time, I realized just how much we needed each other on this long journey.

Aunt Karly let go of me. She turned to Tim and shook hands with him. 'I don't know how I can thank you. Without you, this wouldn't have ended well.'

Tim grinned.

The packed train chugged its way through the dark night. In the overcrowded carriage, I found a spot with Aunt Karly on a bench opposite a Dutch lady with two young children. Auntie knew them from the camp. I wondered where Tim had got to. The carriage was faintly lit by a few oil lamps. I looked at my bundle, which lay in the luggage rack above my head. Just imagine if my things had been left behind at the station: I would have lost my mother's coat!

For a while, I sat half-awake, half-dreaming beside my sleeping aunt. The children and the mother opposite me were also fast asleep. I examined them curiously. They had snuggled up together and were holding each other close. They looked tired, dirty and terribly thin. They could have been paupers! Well, what a thought! Aunt Karly didn't look much better in her worn blue dress with the ragged little white collar and I probably didn't, either. I stared at my dirty fingernails and tried to smooth the creases in my shabby green skirt with my other hand. I looked again at the sleeping family and was overwhelmed by longing for my mother.

It was hot and stuffy in the train. Quietly, I stood up and walked along between the sleeping people and the piles of luggage that stood in the aisle. I pushed open the door to the balcony. It was empty, except for some piled-up suitcases. It was the perfect spot for me to cool down in the dark night. I flopped down on top of a trunk. The cool air felt refreshing, and it was very comforting to hear the train forging ahead along the railway track. Clickety-clack, clickety-clack. We were really on our way. Clickety-clack. Further and further away from my mother, away from the camp. Closer and closer to my father. I was startled out of my thoughts by Tim, who suddenly appeared in front of me.

'Is it alright if I sit next to you?'

'Of course,' I said, and felt myself blush, but luckily you couldn't see that in the dark.

'It's nice and cool here', said Tim, as he sat down beside me on the trunk.

'I know, isn't it lovely? It's the best place during such a long journey at night. It seems to be taking forever.'

'You're not very patient, are you?' he teased.

'Perhaps not.'

'I thought so! What is the height of patience? Well?'

'No idea.'

Tim licked his finger and drew a fish on the side of a dusty suitcase.

'Well?' he asked.

'No idea,' I said again.

'Drawing a fish and waiting for it to swim away.'

It took me a minute to realize what he was saying, and then I laughed out loud. I laughed so much that I couldn't look at his face anymore and had to get up and hold on to the railing of the balcony.

'Well, it wasn't all that funny,' said Tim, when I came back and sat down beside him again on the trunk.

'No, that's true, but it's a long time since anyone told me such a bad joke, so it just really made me laugh.' I had to stop myself from laughing out loud again. 'Before I was in the camp, when I still went to school, there was always someone who wanted to tell a really bad joke and…' I couldn't finish my sentence, all kinds of thoughts shot through my mind.

'I know,' said Tim, moving about restlessly. 'Everything was different then.'

'Yes, everything was different then. I think that's why I had to laugh so much, because of all the years that there wasn't anything to laugh about.'

Tim grinned and then he became serious again. 'I recognize that. Since I was in the men's camp in Ambarawa with my father, nothing is the same anymore.' He pulled a little box from his pocket, opened it, and showed me a gold ring. 'My father's,' he said. 'This is his wedding ring. This is all that's left of him.' He shut the lid of the little box and held it for a moment in his closed hand. Then he put it back in his pocket. 'He asked me to take the ring to my mother.'

I didn't know what to say. 'Is your mother in Surabaya?'

'I hope so,' answered Tim. 'I think so. Nothing is certain. And you? Let me guess. Your mother is dead and you're searching for your father?'

I wanted to ask how he knew that but thought better of it. What did it matter? 'Yes,' I said, 'Karly is my aunt, my father's sister.'

Without saying anything more, we sat next to each other on the balcony. The train thundered along the railway track and slowly ploughed through the night. I thought about Tim's first look, that first second when we looked at each other, and now this strange conversation about our lost parents. A father. A mother. I felt very close to him in this dark night.

When I woke up, it took a moment for me to realize that I was lying with my head on Tim's shoulder, and that he had put his hand over my hand. How long had I been sitting like that? Carefully, I sat up and let go of his hand. Now that he was asleep, I could take a proper look at him. He really did have lots of freckles. I hesitated, took a deep breath and then, very carefully, I traced the outline of his lips. The corners curled up very briefly at my touch, but luckily Tim slept on. I walked back to Aunt Karly and sat down beside her. Outside, dawn was breaking. Palm trees, coconut trees, banana trees, paddy fields and mountains slowly shook off the dark and became visible again. In the train, too, people were coming to life. They stood up, stretched, and collected their things. Aunt Karly had also woken up. She looked at me, groggily.

'Morning,' I said.

'Morning,' said Aunt Karly, yawning. 'Did you sleep well?'

'Quite well.'

'Incredible. Are you sure? I'm shattered.' She looked searchingly at me. 'You're young, that's probably it!'

I felt myself blushing, but I didn't want to tell her that I'd been sitting beside Tim all night.

Huffing and puffing, with its steam whistle screaming, the train slid into the station and came to a halt alongside the platform.

'I want to say goodbye to that young man who helped me,' I announced.

'Alright, we'll wait until most of the people have left the train before we get off,' said Aunt Karly.

'Yes, of course! I don't want to lose you again!' I looked around for Tim. A moment ago, he had been standing on the balcony with his rucksack. He hadn't gone, had he? I couldn't see him on the platform, either. He couldn't have gone! The carriage was almost empty. Now I could get up and look for him without losing sight of Aunt Karly.

'Back in a moment,' I called and ran with my bundle in my hand to the balcony. No Tim! Disappointed, I stopped. This was where we had sat talking last night. I should have kissed him! That thought suddenly made me feel boiling hot and a shudder ran through me. How stupid that I hadn't thought of that until now. I would have finally known what it was really like to kiss a boy.

'Tim, where are you?' I whispered. 'I want to know where you're going in Surabaya.' Perhaps we could see each other again? He couldn't just disappear. I wanted to say goodbye to him.

I leant against the door that opened from the carriage onto the balcony and stared straight ahead. It was then that I saw a small package lying on the floor. It looked just like the little box Tim had shown me last night. It couldn't be! I picked it up off the floor and examined it carefully. Yes, it was Tim's box. I didn't dare open it. This little box with his father's ring was the reason why Tim had made this train journey, and now I was sitting here holding it in my hands. What was I supposed to do?

My aunt came and sat beside me. 'I thought I might find you here. Did you succeed? Did you talk to that young man? What was his name again?'

I shrugged my shoulders and without Aunt Karly noticing, I slid the little box into the pocket of my skirt. 'Tim. He's called Tim. He's disappeared in the crowd!'

'We'll find him. Come on, let's go.' She stepped onto the platform.

I shrugged and followed her off the train. What was I to do? I should have asked for his address. Why hadn't I dared to? But another voice in me objected. Tim shouldn't have just left like that. He should have said goodbye to me. And he should have taken better care of the little box! How could you lose something so valuable on a train? I had to carry on. I had no time to lose. I had to find my father. I didn't have time to go searching for Tim, too.

'Auntie! Auntie! I shouted, 'Wait for me!' and I ran after her down the platform.

LOOKING FOR FATHER

'We're going to look for the Red Cross,' Aunt Karly announced. 'People on the train were saying they have an office here in the station.' She crossed the concourse and seemed to be heading straight for her target. How did she always know exactly what she had to do?

I had to run to keep up with her. 'Do you know where we have to go?'

Auntie didn't answer and strode on. I followed her, swinging my *bungkusan* back and forth. It was wonderful to be moving, to be able to run rather than being stuck in a train. 'Surabaya, here we are again,' and I almost knocked over a lady with my bundle. 'I'm sorry,' I called, and without looking back sprinted after Aunt Karly. I tried to keep my bundle still, which was difficult.

The Red Cross was located in a big room in the left wing of the station. The walls were covered with lists of names, and there were tables piled high with stacks of paper, typewriters, and telephones. It was mostly women working there and you could tell they were from the Red Cross because they wore a sort of uniform. Most of them were wearing trousers and they all wore a grey-blue shirt with a kind of tie. There was a white band with the Red Cross sign around their arms. The room was buzzing with people.

'Why is it so busy here?' I asked.

'They're all people like us, who are hoping to find out more about lost family members,' answered Aunt Karly.

I walked along the lists of names pinned to the walls. 'So many names.'

'Names of people who are missing. Just like your father.'

'No,' I shouted, angrily. 'My father isn't missing! That's like being dead, isn't it? Dad's alive, I know he is!'

'I hope so, too,' she said.

A Red Cross worker came over to us. 'My name is Mrs Pool. Good for you that you found us.' She smiled in a friendly way at us and directed us to one of the tables.

'I'm looking for my father,' I said, as soon as she had sat down. 'I want to know where he is.'

'Of course, you do,' she said, 'but first tell me who you are and where you've come from, so that I can put you on the list of survivors. That way, you'll be registered, so that you can be traced if people turn up looking for you.'

'So, if my father wants to know where I am, and is in touch with the Red Cross, he'll be told that we're in Surabaya?'

'That's the way it's supposed to work,' answered Mrs Pool, cheerfully.

'We came from Ambarawa, camp 9. I'm Karly Arends, twenty-nine years old and this is…'

'Nell Arends. I'm fifteen.'

'Nell is my niece,' Aunt Karly smiled at me. 'Her mother…'

'I'm looking for my father,' I said, quickly. 'My father, Peter Arends, is a captain in the Royal Dutch East Indies Airforce.'

'Peter is my brother,' Auntie added. 'He's a commanding officer in the air force.'

'He left for Tasikmalaya in March 1942.' My throat ached when I said that. 'Do you know where he could be now? Or how I can find him?'

'Let me see. Just a moment.' The woman picked up a list and thumbed through it.

Nervously, I followed every move she made. Each time she turned a page, I tried to read in her face whether it was good or bad news that she was reading in that list that she was scanning. The woman leant forward, took a new list from the piles of paper lying in front of her, went through that one, too, and then laid it down in front of her on the table. 'Your father, as a military man, was probably taken to Japan as a prisoner of war.'

I didn't know what to say to that. Being a Japanese prisoner of war didn't sound good at all.

'I'm going to make enquiries for you, and as soon as we know more about Mr Arends, you'll be informed.' Mrs Pool stood up brusquely, as if indicating that our conversation was over. I must have looked very shocked because when she shook my hand in parting, she said, 'We have many people working in Japan to trace missing people,' and then she went off to talk to some other people.

'It's crazy! I think it's totally crazy!' I shouted, when we were outside again standing in the concourse.

'Yes,' agreed Aunt Karly. 'It's crazy. But I didn't expect anything different. Did you?'

'I don't know. I hadn't expected my father to pop up here in the station of Surabaya straight after our arrival, of course. But an answer like: "He's a prisoner of war in Japan, there you are, off you go." No, I hadn't expected that. And what use was it?'

My aunt shrugged her shoulders. 'Sometimes, you're a real little terror, Nell. What kind of a question is that? They're going to look for your father, and that is more than I dared hope for. Anyway, the Red Cross is really good at finding lost people.'

'But what does that mean? Is he dead or alive? They dropped bombs on Japan, too, didn't they?'

'As far as I'm concerned, your father's alive! Until he's been found, he's alive.' Aunt Karly took my hand and looked at me intensely. 'Don't give up, Nell. Don't give up. You'll see, he'll turn up somewhere, that brother of mine.'

LIVING IN A PROPER HOUSE AGAIN

'How did you get this house, Auntie?' I asked, excitedly. We were walking together through a big, tastefully furnished house in a neighbourhood in the south of the city. It looked just like my grandmother's old house. We had walked there straight after our visit to the Red Cross. 'It's a really lovely house. Furniture, beds, linen and crockery. Everything's here. Only the inhabitants are missing!'

'I know the people who are looking after this house, from before the war,' she answered. 'It's not far from the house where we used to live with Granny. We can't go back there because there are still Japanese people living there.'

'And we're really allowed to stay here? Unbelievable! You have a solution to everything.'

'I wish I did: that would be handy. We've just been lucky. This house has been empty for a few years now. The owner is in Europe, and in the meantime, my Indonesian friends are looking after the house. The valuable things, such as antique furniture, the Chinese porcelain, and the clocks, have been removed and put in storage. The rest has been left for us,' said Aunt Karly. 'Isn't it wonderful?'

'It's more than wonderful!' I shouted, enthusiastically. 'It's fantastic!' I didn't mind at all that we couldn't go back to Granny's house. It would only remind me of my mother. For the first time in years I was back in a proper house! A house with stairs. I ran up to the first floor and threw open the door to the bedroom. 'This is my room!' I jumped up and down a few times on the mattress and then let myself fall headlong onto it.

'Then I'll take the room next to yours,' said Aunt Karly.

I was in bed by seven o'clock. A proper bed with clean sheets that smelt fresh, in a proper house. I had forgotten how lovely that was! I had the bed all to myself. Even if I spread out my arms and legs and stretched as much as I could, I still couldn't touch the edge of the bed. In the camp, I'd only had a narrow strip of mattress of no more than fifty centimetres. And now I didn't just have my own bed, but I also had a whole room all to myself! I had taken my mother's coat out of my bundle and laid it next to my pillow. The coat had a particular scent, and when I smelt that, I felt my mother was very close to me. But now the scent smothered me, and I missed my mother terribly. *Must put it away, then.*

I jumped out of bed and put the coat back in my bundle. Then I picked up my green skirt from the floor and took Tim's box out of the pocket. I opened the box and looked at the gold ring. If only I knew where Tim was, I could take the ring to him. I had to keep this little box safe. I put it in my bundle, put my stuff under the bed and lay down again. I couldn't sleep, even though I was exhausted.

I kept replaying things in my head. The camp, the deserted field where my mother lay, the Japanese guards at the gate, the jostling crowd at Jogjakarta station, the railway tracks that slipped away beneath us as I stood with Tim on the balcony of the train. Where could Tim be right now? He must have felt awful when he discovered that he had lost the ring. If only I knew where he was! I turned over on to my other side. I needed to think of something else. I wanted to sleep. So tired.

In the room next to me, all was quiet. Was my aunt asleep? I could hear the frogs croaking outside. It was a comforting sound. I could also hear the crickets. They chirped louder and louder, as if they were afraid that this would be their last night.

Then I could hear people applauding. Just like the chirping of the crickets, the applause swelled, too… It came from a group of people wearing their Sunday best, standing around the swimming pool. Listen, they were clapping again at the Bandung swimming pool. I was standing on the highest diving-board and listening to all those people who were cheering me on. My mother and father would be so proud if I went from the top diving-board! Just one more jump and I would have my swimming certificate, and then there would be even more applause. I walked forward, stretched my arms, and bent forward. I could see my father and mother standing among the people. They were shouting. I couldn't hear them. It wasn't until I jumped, that I heard them shouting that I shouldn't dive, because there was no water in the swimming pool.

Shivering and covered in sweat, I woke up. I was afraid. It wasn't nice, after all, to sleep all alone in a room. Especially not when you were having a nightmare. My mother had told me that you could chase away a horrible dream, so that it would never come back to torment you again, by going back into your dream to the moment when you had suddenly woken up. But without my mother, I didn't dare do that. I didn't want to go back to the empty swimming pool. I didn't want to go back to my childhood in Bandung. I couldn't bear it. Then everything would start over again. The parting from my father, the camp. I listened to the crickets outside for a moment. It was as if their chirping was becoming grimmer and grimmer. I was scared. I had to get away from here.

I grabbed my pillow and crept to Auntie's room. Carefully, I stuck my head around the door. 'Karly?'

'What's the matter, Nelly?'

'I can't sleep.'

Aunt Karly sat up. 'Neither can I. Those crickets are making such a row.' She turned down the sheets. 'You can come in with me.' In a flash, I was lying beside her. But even next to my aunt, I couldn't sleep, and I tossed and turned restlessly.

'If you just wait quietly, sleep will often come of its own accord. And even if you don't sleep, at least you'll be getting some rest.'

I snuggled up and wrapped my arms around her. 'What's the height of patience, Auntie?'

Aunt Karly didn't answer. She was asleep. I held on to her and thought of Tim.

I was sitting on the veranda of the house and didn't feel like doing anything. In September, here in Surabaya, everything seemed to start with the 'W' of *w*aiting and *w*anting to know. *W*orthless! We had been here for five days now, and there was still no sign of my father.

'You have to be patient,' said Aunt Karly. She always knew exactly what was preoccupying me. She could read me like a book. She set down the teapot and two cups on the table next to me and sat down beside me. 'There's nothing we can do, except walk over to the Red Cross every day to see if there's any news,' she said, while pouring the tea.

'That's true, at least we can ask after him.' I thought of my mother. You couldn't do that with my mother. There was no information point where you could ask how she was getting on in her bamboo coffin in the open field far away from here.

'Mrs Pool of the Red Cross says we have to wait, that we mustn't lose hope, because as long as nothing is definite, everything is possible. Every day, people are returning.'

'Easy to say if you haven't lost anyone. For her, it's completely normal to have thousands of missing people, names that she goes through several times a day. Then she collects new information, which she uses to make new lists, that she hangs on the wall again. I don't want to learn how to wait!' I grumbled, 'I really don't have time for that. There are already enough things I have to learn again.'

'Such as?' Aunt Karly looked at me, curiously.

'Such as almost everything. Being alone and living in a house! That's quite difficult if you haven't done it for a few years. Sleeping on my own in a bed. Clearing up, cooking. I even have to get used to the days themselves. There's not a lot to do here, is there?' I took a sip of tea. 'In the camp everything was fixed, and the day was filled with set tasks and chores.'

'And now there is no-one telling you exactly what to do and exactly when to do it,' she said.

'Yes, and although there's lots I could do, I don't know how to choose. Sometimes, I'm bored. I keep having this feeling that, now that I'm free, there's not a moment to lose, and that I should be putting every minute of the day to good use.'

'Yes, I know… I have the same feeling, and it can be quite confusing with that thought running through your head.'

'And there's no school. Not that school is much fun, but if you can't go there, you don't get to see your friends.'

She nodded. 'Do you remember at the beginning of the war, when you and your mother were living with me and Granny? The schools had already closed, but small groups of pupils used to cycle from one teacher's house to another.'

Of course, I remembered, how we had cycled from teacher to teacher every hour. That had been fun, but when the Japs started putting everyone into camps, that had stopped, too. 'Just imagine, that I could cycle with my friends through Surabaya and could have an hour's tuition anywhere. That would be lovely. At least something would be happening then.' I sighed. If only it were true. There was no school now, and I saw almost no-one. I was bored. I hadn't seen Tim again. Sometimes I met people when I walked with Aunt Karly to the Red Cross office. I always asked whether they knew Tim, and if they had seen him. So far, without any luck. He was as untraceable as my father.

A few days later, I found two bikes. They had been stowed somewhere at the back of the veranda.

'Now I can go into town,' I cried, enthusiastically.

'Don't you dare,' said Aunt Karly, firmly. 'You are not going to town on your own, and you are certainly not going to go off on your own on a bike. Before you know it, you'll come across the youths who are fighting for an independent Indonesia. You don't want to run into those *Pemudas* if you're a girl.'

As if I would go anywhere near those guys! 'I don't think they're that dangerous,' I said. 'And if I take the bike, I can cycle off if necessary. So, it's quite alright for me to go out.' I wanted to cycle around to find Tim. That was all. But Aunt Karly wouldn't let me. So, I carried on being bored; that is, until I found a case with a sewing machine in the wardrobe in my bedroom.

'How wonderful!' said Aunt Karly, when I showed it her. 'I used to have one like that in Granny's house. I made lots of things on it.'

'So, you know how it works?'

Aunt Karly nodded and looked the machine over.

'There's also a sewing box in the wardrobe where the machine was,' I said enthusiastically and ran upstairs. I was back in a moment. 'I've got pins, needles and a pair of scissors, and some white cloth with blue dots.'

'A piece of fabric with polka dots, and it looks as if there's just enough to make a nice dress.'

'Is it difficult to make a dress?'

'No, not very. I'll teach you if you want.'

'Please,' I cried, excitedly. 'Preferably now. Anything is better than being bored.'

Aunt Karly looked at the machine. She threaded the machine and sewed a little seam on a spare piece of cloth she had found in the case. We cut the material and pinned it, and then she gave me instructions. 'You have to sew these two pieces of cloth together on the machine.'

'I hope it works,' I cried, as I guided the material with both hands under the presser foot of the machine, and Aunt Karly turned the crank. I'd never done this before, and my hands were shaking. The needle went up and down so fast. 'Stop! It's veering off to the side.'

Aunt Karly held the crank still and examined my needlework.

'That looks fine, Nell. Just keep going.'

'Can we go slower?'

'Of course,' said Auntie, as she started turning the crank again.

I guided the material through the sewing machine, and it was only now that I could see properly how the needle went up and down through the cloth making even stitches, all precisely the same size.

'I'd like us to make something together every single day. We make a good team!' I said.

It was a great project, that dress of mine. And it was nice to be learning something new. We had been working at it for a few days when my aunt snipped off the last little bit of loose thread.

'Done! Try it on, Nell!'

I pulled the dress over my head. Delightedly, I felt the soft material with my hands and did a pirouette. The skirt swished out.

'I've never had such a beautiful dress.' I stopped in front of my aunt and gave her a kiss. 'Thank you, dear, dear Auntie.'

'Your mother would have loved it,' she said, wistfully.

'I made it myself! She would have thought that was the best part,' I answered happily, and let my skirt swish around again. 'And so, it is! Now a dress for you, Auntie!'

'I don't need one.'

'I really want to make another one!'

'There's no more material, Nell.'

GIRL OUT OF PLACE

On 12th September, coming from the Red Cross office with Aunt Karly, I ran into Lisa. There had been no news of my father, of course. I was beginning to worry about whether he was still alive. Or perhaps he was alive, but couldn't remember who he was, and was lost somewhere in Japan? If he'd lost his memory, how could he find his way home? And if he stayed away much longer, I might not recognize him anymore. That particular day, I'd left the Red Cross office, and was standing near the entrance to the station waiting for Aunt Karly, when out of the blue I saw a familiar face coming toward me: it was Lisa!

I was so glad to see her. 'Where were you? I looked everywhere for you when I left the camp, but I couldn't find you anywhere.'

'I was with my mother. She was ill.'

'Nothing serious, I hope. How long have you been here in Surabaya?'

'Since the end of August,' answered Lisa. 'With my mother.'

'Me too, we could have bumped into each other earlier.'

Lisa shrugged her shoulders. 'I don't know. Perhaps. My mother was taken to the hospital here.'

'How is she now?' Stupid question. I saw the grief in her eyes. I could have bitten off the tip of my tongue. I shouldn't have asked that because it never ended well for mothers who were ill.

'She died a week ago. Buried two days ago,' murmured Lisa.

'Oh no, how awful!'

'I'm glad you asked. You're the only one. Everyone either avoids the subject or takes a wide berth around me. It was probably the same for you.'

Confused, I nodded. I could see the tears in Lisa's eyes and didn't know what to say.

'I live with my aunt now,' sighed Lisa.

'Me too.' I could see a sparkle reappearing in Lisa's eyes. She grabbed my arm. 'We should do something together. Why don't you come out with me? We're going to visit the De Wit family later. With the twins.'

'Do you mean Jo and Trudy, who were in our kitchen shift?'

'Yes, they're all together again in their house in Surabaya; father, mother, the brothers and the twins. Will you come? Perhaps your aunt wants to come, too?'

'Come where?' asked Aunt Karly, as she approached us. 'Lisa, it's so good to see you.'

'To the De Wit family,' explained Lisa. 'I'm going there in a little while with my aunt.'

'Sorry, I can't go,' said Aunt Karly, decisively.

Disappointed, I looked at her. What did she have to do that was so important? I couldn't think of anything. She probably just didn't feel like visiting them.

'But if you drop Nell back home after the visit and she's back before evening, she can go.'

Relieved, I kissed my aunt and laughed. I wasn't that desperate to visit the De Wit family, but I really wanted to hang out with Lisa. To do something different. Perhaps to run into Tim somewhere?

It was a twenty-minute walk from the station to the De Wit house. Lisa and I walked behind her aunt. We didn't say much. That was the nice thing about Lisa. You could be together without having to talk. I was hot from walking, but I didn't mind. It was wonderful to be going somewhere.

'I don't really know Jo or Trudy very well,' I said, as we walked into the De Wit's house.

'Me neither!' retorted Lisa, laughing.

It was really nice at the De Wit's house. There was lemonade and Mrs De Wit had baked some cookies, which we finished off in no time. Everyone talked at once. The youngest boys ran around the house. Mr and Mrs De Wit were fine with everything. Everyone enjoyed just being together again. The twin sisters, Jo and Trudy, kept shouting about how happy they were that we had come. They said it so often, that I couldn't bear it anymore. They seemed to have everything that anyone could wish for, and meanwhile I didn't even know if I would ever see my father again.

I went out into the garden and found Lisa at the bottom near a group of tamarind trees. 'I thought you might be somewhere out here in the garden.'

'Why?'

'Because it's unbearable to watch, isn't it? All that family togetherness. It must be upsetting you, too.'

Lisa nodded, but didn't say anything. I was sure that we were both thinking of our mothers.

'But it's also nice that they all found each other again,' I said, to break the silence.

Lisa closed her eyes for a moment. 'What do you mean?'

'Well, it doesn't work out that way for everyone, does it, that everything turns out alright?'

'No,' said Lisa. 'Look at me. My mother is dead.'

'So is mine,' I said. 'Dead as doornails.' And that made us both laugh really loudly. I laughed so much, that the tears poured down my cheeks. It felt like a release. Not because it was so funny, but because I had already cried so much about the death of my mother, that it was great to do something completely different for a change and to laugh about it. I felt closer to Lisa in our mutual sorrow, than to the De Wit family and their happiness.

'It's so nice to laugh together!' As I said that, I thought of the last time I had laughed that much. That had been with Tim on the train. I told Lisa how Tim had hauled me onto the train from Jogjakarta to Surabaya, and how I had lain flat out on the balcony, as the train pulled out of the station. I didn't tell her how nice it had been to sit next to him on that night train and to listen to his silly jokes. I also kept quiet about the box Tim had lost on the train. But I did tell her that I had, more or less, lost Tim and didn't know where he lived.

'If I were you, I'd go to Hotel Oranje some time. Lots of people go there. And if he isn't there himself, there might be people who do know him.'

'Good idea. I really want to see him again.'

'I hope you find him,' said Lisa, 'because I think you're in love with him.'

'I am not!' I felt the blood rushing to my face. Was I really in love with Tim?

NEWS OF MY FATHER

'I have good news for you,' said Mrs Pool, one morning. It was the 19th September and it was the twenty-fifth time that we had gone to enquire if there was any news of my father. Mrs Pool opened a drawer and pulled out a box with alphabetically filed letters. Skilfully, her fingers moved through the box. 'We received these letters through the Red Cross in Nagasaki.' She pulled out one envelope from among the others and gave it to Aunt Karly. 'I haven't read the letter, but your father is definitely still alive,' she said to me. 'That has been confirmed by the Red Cross in Nagasaki. He's still a long way away, but he's alive!'

I jumped up from my chair and felt like singing. But then I realized what it meant. Yes, he was still alive, but so far away, in Japan! That was a big disappointment. I wanted to rip open that letter right away and read it, but Aunt Karly was much calmer about these things.

She thanked Mrs Pool politely for taking care of everything and put the envelope into her bag. 'We're going to read that letter in our own good time when we get home, Nell. Are you coming?'

'I want to know what's in that letter now!' I cried, when we had left the Red Cross office. But my aunt flatly refused. 'You don't read something like that in the street. We'll wait until we get home.'

Crossly, I walked with her out of the station, along the tram tracks, past the hospital, the empty school, until we arrived at our house.

'Open it, open it!' I cried, as soon as we were inside. Excitedly, I pulled at her arm.

'No!' she said. She was holding the letter out in her hand.

'Why not?' I asked, angrily.

'Because you are going to do that by yourself. That's why.'

'My father didn't write it to me.'

'Because your father wasn't to know how grown-up you are now.'

'You're his sister.'

'And you're his daughter, Nelly, and that's why you have to read that letter first, and I'm going to go and visit my Indonesian friends. Perhaps they've been to the market, maybe they've bought us some food at the *pasar*. I'll be back soon.' Aunt Karly laid the envelope on the table and disappeared.

I sat down at the table and rested my head on my hands. I stared at the envelope for a long time. There wasn't anything unusual about it. Rectangular. Off-white paper. Sealed. No stamp. My mother's name written in blue ink: 'To Elenore Arends-Parson'. I took a sharp knife from the drawer of the table. I hesitated for a moment, and then carefully slit open the envelope. I put the knife back in the drawer and sat holding the opened envelope in my hand. Then I sighed and pulled the paper from the envelope. The letter was short.

My dearest Elenore,

I hope you and our Cornelia …

I couldn't go on. My eyes refused to focus on the words. I could only see black blotches on the white paper. I realized, that because of the death of my mother, *"our Cornelia"* had ceased to exist. I was now only my father's *"Cornelia"*. My hands shook. I laid the letter on the table and sat on my hands to stop them shaking. I took a deep breath and carried on reading:

I hope you and our Cornelia have survived the war at my mother's in Surabaya. I long to see you both again, but first I have to try to get away from here. Everything here has been destroyed because of the bomb and everyone is on the run. I hope to catch a ride on a plane out of here shortly. See you soon.

A kiss for Nelly. My love to you both.

Yours,

Peter

I sat at the table and couldn't move. That's how Aunt Karly found me when she came back. She stood behind me, wrapped her arms around me, and held me tight.

'He doesn't know a thing,' I sobbed. 'Not about the camp, not that Granny isn't here anymore, and not about my mother, not about us.'

'We will have to write to let him know, and it's best that you do that.'

'I can't. I can't write to him about my mother. He might think it's my fault that she fell ill.'

'Of course not! Don't say such silly things. I know it's hard to write to him, I realize that. Grief is blacker than ink.'

'My father might wish that it was me who had died instead of my mother.'

'Stop, Nell. You're not to say that ever again! Do you hear me? You mustn't think that. Your father adores you.'

'Does he?' I shouted, trembling with rage. The pent-up fury of the last few months found a way out. 'And where is he now, then, this father of mine? Why did he have to go and be a pilot, so that he wasn't here when my mother and I needed him? If he loved me so much, why couldn't he have stayed with us in America? My mother would still have been alive then! He can stay in Japan for all I care!' I ran out of the room and slammed the door behind me.

That evening, I stayed in my room, and I didn't patch things up with Aunt Karly. I wanted the oblivion of sleep so that I didn't have to think about anything anymore, but it took a long time to fall asleep. I dreamt of my father. He was inspecting airplane factories in America, and my mother and I were travelling with him. I was walking with my mother in the Grand Canyon on a narrow path that lead between the strangely shaped rocks. It was very hot, but my mother was wearing the beautiful woollen coat, that my father had just given her.

'Your father will be here in a minute,' said my mother, and not long afterwards, he came driving towards us in a big Ford and beeped the horn when he saw us. The car stopped beside us. The door opened and my mother got in. My father beeped the horn again, gave me the thumbs up, revved the engine, and tore off with my mother. I was left there, all alone, just watching the car drive off into the distance.

MERDEKA

'Where are you? Where are you?' Dawn had just broken, and I was sitting up in bed. Who was shouting like that in my room? I was sure I could hear someone, and it took me a while to realize, that it was my own voice that had woken me up. For a moment, I didn't know where I was. Was I travelling with my mother? No, of course not. It was just a horrible dream.

I had to get up, but I didn't want to. Today, I had to write to my father. No idea how to go about it. Why was it taking so long for my life to get back to normal again? I had thought it would be fun to live here, but I was incredibly bored, because I was stuck at home so much. Aunt Karly still wouldn't let me go off on my own, but I wanted to get out of the house. I wanted to cycle around the city again, to meet friends and chat with them about normal things. About the nicest kind of tea to buy and whose birthday was next, about boys and who had already been kissed, and by whom. I was fed up with all the sad and boring things. I pulled the sheet over my head. I wasn't here. I didn't want to be here. I wasn't going to write that letter. I turned over a few times, lay on my stomach and put my head under the pillow.

Suddenly, in the dark, the vision of my father in his Ford reappeared. He gave me the thumbs up and drove off again with my mother. I was left behind, alone. *Mustn't think about that.* I pulled the pillow off my head and took a deep breath. Then I jumped out of bed. I didn't want to give in to my depressed mood, so I pulled on the new dress with the polka dots that I had made with Aunt Karly. That dress always cheered me up. Then I wrapped a red scarf, that I had found in a wardrobe, around my unruly curls, and to cheer myself up even more, I turned a pirouette in the middle of my room. I promptly fell over and immediately felt a whole lot better.

'What on earth are you doing?' called Aunt Karly from the room next to me.

'Nothing! I'm writing stupid letters to even more stupid fathers, because my stupid Auntie says I have to.'

I heard her laughing as she went downstairs. I laid out pen and paper, but just as I was about to start, my inspiration disappeared. I held the pen in my hand and stared miserably at the paper. My thumb and finger were already covered in ink. I just couldn't write that my mother was dead. As soon as I put those words down on paper, she would be even deader than she already was, far away in the field behind the Ambarawa camp. But I couldn't give up now: I had to try. An hour later, I had got two sentences down on paper.

Surabaya, 20th September 1945

Dear Dad,

I'm in Surabaya with Aunt Karly.

The Red Cross knows where we are.

Love Nelly.

It wasn't much, but it was an answer. There was a black thumb print on the paper, but there was no way I was going to write that letter again. I put the sheet into an envelope and ran downstairs.

'Done!' I yelled, and waved the letter around. Aunt Karly didn't react. She had fallen asleep in her chair on the veranda. The book she had been reading, lay in her lap. I didn't want to wake her, and I didn't want to wait. If Auntie was asleep, I could just quickly go and post the letter. I hesitated for a moment. Surely, she wouldn't mind if I took the letter that had taken so much effort round to the Red Cross?

I grabbed one of the bikes that was stowed at the back of the veranda and took it outside. Then I looked once more at my aunt, but she was still asleep. I hesitated before shutting the gate behind me. Not long afterwards, I was cycling down the road, my heart thumping. It was wonderful to pedal a bike again for the first time in years. I was twelve years old again, and free! I cycled fast and soon reached Hotel Oranje. It was really busy in the street. What could be going on? I was about to stop to have a look when I thought better of it and cycled on. I wanted to post that letter first. When I got to the Red Cross office, I parked my bike and handed in my letter. I was sweaty and breathless from pedalling so hard. I wanted to cycle straight back to Hotel Oranje, but then decided it was so close I might as well walk, so I left the bike there and ran back to the square. It was incredibly busy. There were never usually that many people out in the streets. I let myself be carried along by the crowd to the hotel. Could Tim be here somewhere, too? Lisa had said that he might occasionally go to Hotel Oranje.

An older lady wearing a hat pointed angrily at the roof of the hotel where the Dutch flag was flying and grumbled: 'They've gone mad. They shouldn't fly that flag. It's extremely dangerous to be so provocative!'

'Why not? The war is over!' screamed a young woman next to me. I hurried past the entrance to Hotel Oranje. Once, when my father had just left for the war and we had moved in with Granny in Surabaya, I had gone for tea there with my mother. I stopped. *'Keep moving,'* a voice inside me said. *'Don't hang about here!'* but I was tempted to have a quick look in the hotel, so I turned around, walked back to the entrance, and went inside.

At first it seemed empty and much cooler than outside. But as I walked into the lobby, I found it was full of people. The Indonesian hotel staff were running back and forth among a crowd of excited Europeans. Most of the men were my father's age, and there were hardly any women. I could see immediately that Tim wasn't among them, and I didn't recognize anyone else. Perhaps I should ask someone if they knew Tim? I hesitated, but I knew I had to get going. In the left-hand corner of the lobby, aside from the crowd, a gentleman was sitting in a large armchair. He had short hair, big ears that stood out from his head a little, and he was wearing conspicuous black-framed glasses. Just as I was gathering the courage to go up to him, a group of men came running down the stairs, shouting. They quickly ran straight back up the stairs, pursued by some of the men from the lobby. I took a step back, closed my eyes and took a deep breath.

'I don't think you should be here!'

Startled, I opened my eyes. The man in the armchair was now standing next to me and was looking at me sternly. I broke out in a sweat. 'I... I'm looking for a boy. His name is Tim. Do you... do you know him by any chance?' I stammered, my face burning. 'Tim Thissen. He's supposed to be here.'

The man shook his head. 'No, I'm sorry. I don't know that name. I don't know your boyfriend.' He had an unpleasant nasal voice.

'He's not my boyfriend!' I had the urge to laugh but I didn't dare because the man was still glaring at me.

'Well, I haven't seen your brother, either. And you'd better be off back home to your mother, because it's definitely not safe here today for little girls. D'you understand? I was born here, and I've lived in the Dutch East Indies for fifty years now, but I've never experienced anything like this. First the Japs lock us up in camps, and now this. Soekarno and Hatta want independence – for us to become the Republic of Indonesia! But we can't accept that!' He looked at me angrily. *'Merdeka!* What on earth are they thinking? Collaborating with those Japs, they were good at that, and now they're just firing shots at will. So be off with you. It's too dangerous here. There's going to be serious trouble because they want us out of the Indies.' The man gasped for breath. His lips were purplish and moist.

I didn't know how to react so I ran out as fast as I could. "Home to my mother." How dare he! I didn't even have a mother anymore. And what was I doing in there, anyway? There were so many boys of Tim's age in Surabaya. It would be too much of a coincidence if someone there actually knew him.

Outside Hotel Oranje, an even bigger crowd had formed. There was a group of men standing on the roof of the hotel. They were shouting loudly, and I looked at them with surprise. Was it the same group that had been running up and down the stairs? What was going on? All of a sudden, Indonesian freedom fighters appeared, waving flags, and screaming: *'Merdeka!'* 'Freedom or die!' And then things started happening quickly. A man I didn't know grabbed my hand and dragged me across the street. There was a lot of shouting and shots were fired. I was scared to look back at the hotel but when I did, the Dutch flag had been replaced with the Indonesian one. Furious Indonesian freedom fighters had ripped the blue band off the Dutch flag, leaving only the red and white stripes.

Right in front of me a fight had broken out in the street between Indonesian *Pemudas* and Europeans.

'Get out of here!' the stranger cried and he dragged me away from the brawling in front of the hotel before vanishing into the crowd. I was shaking all over. I wished I hadn't come. *Quick! Hurry up! Go home*! I ran back to the Red Cross office. That was where I'd left my bike, wasn't it? Everything started to spin around me. I leant against the wall and slowly slid to the ground. My bike had gone.

'What's got into you? You're not a child anymore!' shouted Aunt Karly when I finally returned to the house late in the afternoon.

'I'm sorry about the bike.'

'Losing a bike is one thing, but have you any idea how worried I've been?' She disappeared up to her own room and I didn't hear a thing from her all evening. Restlessly, I roamed the house. Auntie was sort of right, but the letter to my father had been posted. I didn't tell her how brilliant it had been to cycle around Surabaya on my own, and to be in the square among all those people. Being a witness to those events made me feel that something important was happening.

A day after the fighting at Hotel Oranje, Aunt Karly was still mad at me.

'I don't want you wandering the streets on your own. Is that perfectly clear? You could have died and what would I say to your father, then?'

'I'm sorry, Auntie. I won't do it again.'

'You'd better not. Next time, you might not be so lucky.'

'Do you think we're going to get that independent Indonesian Republic?' I asked, carefully.

'I didn't know you were interested in politics.'

'People are talking about it out there. At Hotel Oranje, I heard that the Netherlands won't accept Soekarno's declaration of independence, and that lots of young Indonesians are prepared to fight for the republic.'

'Yes, exactly, Nell. The Netherlands aren't going to make a gift of independence, and now that those guys have the support of the Japanese, they are roaming the streets. The Japanese commander has given them access to the city armouries, and you're old enough to understand what that means.'

'How do you know that?'

'I have my sources. So, you're not to go off on your own anymore. Is that clear?'

'I can't just sit inside all day! If you don't want me to go off on my own, then come with me. We really need to go to the Red Cross to see if my letter to my father has reached Japan.'

'What nonsense, Nell! You can't expect an answer to your letter within a day. That's going to take a while. We're not going out. I won't have it! There's rioting and looting going on everywhere, so it's too dangerous out in the streets.'

Aunt Karly's words scared me, but I didn't want to admit that. 'They're not going to rob our house if we go out for a little while.'

Aunt Karly sighed. I didn't give in. 'Of course there won't be an answer to my letter yet, but I want to see if we can find my bike at the Red Cross office, and once we're there, we might as well ask in case there's some other message from my father.'

'Alright, you win,' she relented. 'We'll go and make

enquiries one more time.'

And so, once again, we made our way to the Red Cross office. My bike was nowhere to be found and there was no news of my father.

Mrs Pool of the Red Cross tried to cheer me up. 'Your father is on his way. More and more people are coming back from Japan, it just takes time. As soon as your father lands on Java, we'll be in touch with you.'

I hardly responded to Mrs Pool's words. I felt it was silly to have bothered her again, but I couldn't rid myself of my disappointment. Aunt Karly thanked Mrs Pool, put her arm through mine and pulled me out of the building. Silently, I walked beside my aunt: I didn't feel like talking.

Normally, I loved getting out of the house, but now I just wanted to go home and cry. Aunt Karly took no notice. 'You have to keep your head above the water and carry on swimming. Never give up, Nelly. That bike is not going to come back, but your father is, I know that for sure. There is such a thing as fate, or karma.' She strode on. I could hardly keep up. 'Your father has an incredible force of spirit and that's going to bring him back here to Java. You shouldn't fret but look forward to that day. We have someone who really belongs with us, someone to look forward to seeing again. You should cherish that. It just needs more time. That's what I keep telling myself: something like that takes time.'

I tried to keep up with her, but my thoughts were jumping in all directions. Aunt Karly knew what she was talking about. Stupid of me. I blushed when I realized that I wasn't the only one who had lost people. Aunt Karly's fiancée, Chris, had been killed in the first days of the battle of Java. He had been shot at from a Japanese plane while he was laying dynamite to blow up a bridge. And just after that, Granny died. My aunt had never complained about those things, never even spoken of them. And my mother had been her best friend. Now the only family she had, apart from me, was her brother, my father. I put my arm around her and hugged her in the middle of the street. 'I'm sorry, Auntie. You're right. I mustn't whine. It doesn't matter that it's taking so long for Dad to come back, just so long as he does come back.'

Aunt Karly linked arms with me again. 'And he will! And as soon as that father of yours is here again, I want to go to Holland.' She said that last thing softly, almost in a whisper as if she didn't dare say it out loud, but although I'd heard her, I pretended I hadn't. There was no way I was going to go to the Netherlands, but I couldn't bear the thought of losing my aunt too. I stayed quiet for some time.

'A penny for your thoughts?' she asked.

BERSIAP: BE PREPARED

Following that last trip to the Red Cross office, we hardly left the house. Mostly, we stayed on the veranda where it was cool. And if we did go out, it was never for long and we always stayed as close to the house as possible. The days seemed to run into each other. They all seemed the same. The heat was oppressive, and so was the boredom. It stayed that way until Ludo, Lisa's cousin, suddenly appeared on our doorstep on 15th October. His visit finally woke me up.

'I've been sent to fetch you and escort you to our house,' said Ludo, gaily. 'Today, we're having a party because our Lisa has turned fifteen. If you both come, there'll be fifteen guests. That will bode well for Lisa in the coming year. So, ladies, how about it?'

I jumped up. Instantly, the tiredness of the last few weeks disappeared. It had stemmed from the utter boredom which had paralyzed me to such an extent that all I'd done was slouch on the veranda.

'Yes! Yes!' I shouted, excitedly. 'At last, something is going to happen in this godforsaken city!' I grabbed Ludo's hands and danced around the room with him.

GIRL OUT OF PLACE

'Out of the question,' called Aunt Karly. 'What on earth are you thinking? It's extremely dangerous to go into town.'

'Please, Aunt Karly! Oh, please!' I let go of Ludo and dragged Auntie across the veranda. I tried to dance her around the room, but she resisted, stiffly, so nothing much came of my attempt to cheer her up.

'Do come, please, ma'am,' said Ludo, and he took hold of Karly and danced a few steps with her. It made her laugh. 'I don't know.' Despairingly, she put her hands up in the air and then let them drop again.

'Please, dear Auntie, please, may we? Do say yes!' I begged. 'You won't regret it. If we stay here, we'll be so bored!' My plea fell on deaf ears. She didn't react. Desperately, I tried to attract her attention and stood in front of her, grabbed her hands and jumped up and down. Limply, she let her arms move with me, but she still didn't answer.

'Oh, do say yes! You're invited too!' said Ludo. 'We live only a few streets away and I know a shortcut to our house. I can find the way blindfold. It won't be dangerous at all.'

Fortunately, my aunt relented. Again, she put her hands up in the air: 'Alright, alright, I give up. I'll come.'

'You are a darling, Auntie. You're a darling!'

'You'll make Lisa really happy,' answered Ludo, delightedly.

'And me too,' I said, as I ran in from the veranda. 'Let me just dress up a bit for Lisa. Back in a second.'

'Hurry up, won't you?' called Auntie and Ludo together.

'It's wonderful that you're here!' Lisa beamed at me. She was wearing the blue velvet ribbon that I had brought her in her hair. The colour matched her eyes beautifully. Her fingers played with the ends of the ribbon. I was pleased that I had been able to find something to give her. A birthday without presents isn't a proper birthday at all. Even in the camp, you were always given something. Usually something edible like an extra spoonful of sugar. My mother gave me a handkerchief once, that she had embroidered herself. *Mustn't think about that now.*

Together, we'd all just sung 'Happy Birthday' for Lisa – Aunt Karly, Ludo, the three aunts and the nine cousins (four girls, five boys). And then we had warm lemonade and cake. I was sitting with Lisa on a porch swing, in the furthest corner of the veranda, where you could feel a gentle breeze. The others were sitting around the table in wicker chairs. The veranda was full of life, love, and light. Everyone was relaxed and happy. I'd forgotten that birthdays made you so merry. I couldn't get used to it.

'I'm so glad you're here, Nelly,' said Lisa.

'Me too. So nice to see you again.'

'Now it's really a proper birthday!'

'Absolutely! And at last something good's happening. Have you been bored these last few weeks, too? It's unbelievable! There's absolutely nothing, a zillion times nothing to do, if you're not allowed to go anywhere.'

'So, you're not allowed out, either? I'm glad!'

'I'm not! It's really stupid,' I protested.

'I mean I'm glad I'm not the only one who has to stay at home!'

'Why didn't you say so!' I laughed.

'I did say so!' Lisa's voice sounded a bit croaky. 'I'm glad it's my birthday. That way you get to go out and I get to see you.' She reached for my hand and as we looked at each other, we started laughing again.

'Nice to hear such laughter again. It chases away the evil spirits,' said Lisa's aunt, and she poured us another glass of warm lemonade. 'Now that it's available, you must drink plenty.'

'We will, Auntie,' answered Lisa, 'I could drink three of your jugs of lemonade.'

Lisa's aunt went to sit with Aunt Karly and the others. Lisa and I rocked gently to and fro on the porch swing.

'My life is so incredibly dull!' I complained.

'Not as dull as mine. You went looking for Tim, saw the *Pemudas* and had an adventure on the bike.'

'You mean I lost the bike and didn't find Tim. And then I went to the Red Cross with Auntie one more time, and after that we stayed home.'

'Any news of your father?'

'No. Everyone says he's on his way, but it's taking forever. Aunt Karly says I'm impatient.' I shrugged my shoulders. 'Do you know what the height of patience is? Tim asked me that question on the train to Surabaya.'

'Still in love?'

I couldn't help blushing. 'Of course not. I just like him.' I felt myself turning even redder.

'I'll test you! Do you remember what he looks like?' asked Lisa. 'What is his hair like?'

'Long dark hair which sticks out in all directions.'

'That was easy. Now a more difficult question. Eyes?'

I thought of Tim. It was as if he was standing in front of me. 'Hazel eyes with white flecks.'

'Nose?'

'Small and freckled.' And before she could ask anymore, I said: 'and a cute mouth with lips that curl up at the corners.'

Lisa looked at me closely. 'If you can remember everything about him that well, then you either have a photographic memory or you're in love! Obviously, you're in love. You just have to be patient. You're bound to see him again. Just like you're going to find your father again.'

'Patience!' I shouted, angrily. 'Don't you start on about that, too. Do you know what the height of patience is? Drawing a fish and waiting for it to swim away.'

'In love, just like I said. The height of patience for you is more like — thinking of Tim and waiting for him to pop up.'

I laughed, but not very convincingly. 'Or writing a letter to my father and waiting for him to return. Compared to that, waiting for a fish is easy.'

'No, seriously, Nell. If it's meant to be, Tim will cross your path again.'

'Says who?'

'Says me,' said Lisa. 'You'll see, he'll surface and then your life will start moving again.' She pushed against the floor with her foot and the porch seat started swinging to and fro again.

'What a lovely afternoon,' sighed my aunt when we left Lisa's house at around four o'clock. We'd thanked everyone several times and said goodbye, and I had promised Lisa that I would visit her again at the very first chance. Now Auntie and I were on our way home together with Ludo. There was a pleasant breeze and there were other people in the streets who were out enjoying the fresh air, too.

'I really enjoyed that party,' said Aunt Karly. 'For a moment, it felt as if all my worries had simply vanished.'

'I'm glad that I convinced you to come!' said Ludo, gaily.

'Convinced me? I fully intended to go with you. We're at home enough as it is, and you can't miss a birthday. You have to celebrate that, especially when you never know how long life will be! And we are in good hands with you.'

It took a lot of effort not to laugh at my aunt. She probably had to overcome a lot of fears to go out with all the trouble on the streets these days.

'I'll make sure I get you home safely,' said Ludo, and he set off at a brisk pace.

We walked on without saying much, each wrapped up in their own thoughts. I was thinking about Lisa and her positive outlook on life. I thought about what she had said about me and Tim; that if it was meant to be, we would meet again. I wasn't so sure. I wasn't as optimistic as Lisa.

I was rudely awakened from my daydreaming when Ludo suddenly shouted: 'We've got to get out of here!' He was deathly pale and dragged us into an alley, swearing, and pushed us up against the houses there. From the alley way I saw a truck come tearing up. It stopped in the middle of the street with the engine roaring. Young Indonesian men jumped down from the back. I estimated their age at not more than sixteen, at the most seventeen. They were wearing bandanas and open shirts. Most of them were armed with bamboo sticks with a sharpened point. One or two had a gun. They were shouting and waving their weapons around aggressively, and I glimpsed how they ran into the houses, dragged the inhabitants out and chased them onto the truck.

I stood flattened against a house with Aunt Karly and watched how the *Pemudas* randomly rounded up white men in the streets and forced them to get onto the back of the truck. I could feel my aunt holding her breath. I couldn't stop shaking. Aunt Karly grabbed my hand, but the tension in my body wouldn't go away.

'We have to get away from here,' said Ludo. 'I didn't expect them to make a raid around here!' He was standing on the other side of my aunt and slowly he pulled her along the houses, away from the truck. 'This way, Nell,' said Auntie softly. My back was covered in cold sweat, but I didn't move. I wanted to run away, but my legs wouldn't work.

Aunt Karly pulled my arm. 'Come on, Nell. We have to get out of here!'

I knew she was right and that it was dangerous to stay there, but I carried on watching the freedom fighters, who kept rounding up more and more men and boys.

Then I saw Tim. 'No, it can't be true,' I whispered, but it was really him. Tim was among the boys who were being rounded up and thrown onto the back of the truck, together with about twenty other men. His right eye was shut and there was blood coming from his nose.

'No!' I shouted, furiously. 'No, not Tim. You can't just take him away like that!' Sick with fear, I pulled free from Aunt Karly, ran out of the alley way, and tried to get closer to the truck, onto which people were still being thrown. 'Tim! Tim,' I screamed. Now that I had finally found him, I didn't want him to be driven away on that truck. I had to give him the ring. I wanted to —

Ludo quickly ran after me, grabbed my arm, and pulled me back to the side of the street.

'Have you gone mad?' he shouted. 'Do you want to be rounded up by those guys? You can't do that, Nell! You don't think they'll go easy on girls, do you?'

I shook my head. Of course, I didn't want to be taken away, but I did want to help Tim. The doors of the truck slammed. A final freedom fighter jumped in and shouted: *'Belanda Tabe*, bye bye Dutchman.' With squealing tyres, the truck took off.

Tim was standing at the back of the loading space, hanging half-way out over the ramp.

In desperation, I put my hands in the air. 'I'm here, Tim!' I screamed. At last he saw me.

'What are you doing here, Nell?' But he was beaten back down with a bamboo stick and disappeared into the bottom of the loading space. A moment later, he was standing up straight again and shouted: 'Listen to the radio! You've got to listen to the radio!'

Then the truck sped away and Tim fell back to the bottom of the vehicle again.

'Nell! You've got to come with me now!' ordered Ludo, yanking me by the arm. But I didn't move.

'We must get out of here!' repeated Ludo. I looked down the street once more in the direction of where the truck had gone, and then Ludo dragged me back to Aunt Karly. She was furious.

'What is the matter with you?' she said. 'You could have been killed! How could you do that?' Her voice sounded shrill and her hands were trembling. I couldn't respond.

'Answer me!' she shouted as she took hold of me with two hands and shook me. Then she suddenly let go and her hands dropped by her side. 'I'm sorry, Nell, I'm sorry. I didn't mean to be so angry. I was just really frightened.'

'Tim was one of them,' I whispered, my voice choking.

'Tim?' asked Aunt Karly. 'Are you sure?'

I nodded. 'He was one of the boys they threw onto the truck.'

Aunt Karly didn't answer immediately. She held me for a moment.

'We really must get moving. It's too dangerous to stay here.' Ludo's voice sounded strained. In silence, we followed him.

When we had gone far enough, Auntie said: 'It will be alright. Those boys have all just been released from the camps, I'm sure they won't lock them up again.'

She wanted to reassure me, but I heard the hesitation in her voice. I was worried about Tim. *Pemudas* weren't allowed to just round people up, and yet they were doing it. Who was to say whether they would release those prisoners? And why did Tim have to end up in the back of that truck, just when I had found him again? Lisa said that, if it was meant to be, then Tim would cross my path again. So, was it also meant to be, that I'd lose him again, just when I had found him?

WE HAVE TO GET AWAY FROM HERE

'Let's switch on the radio,' I said, as soon as we got home. I walked into the sitting room to where the radio stood on a small table.

'It's a miracle there's still a radio in this house. Look at that – what a magnificent machine!'

I nodded. My aunt was right. It was a beautifully designed big black Bakelite model, with speakers on both sides. We had never turned it on before.

Aunt Karly squatted in front of the radio. 'I think it's this knob.' She turned the left of the three black knobs at the bottom of the receiver. A light came on behind a narrow strip of glass, and we could see the numbers for the stations.

'It works!' I shouted, excitedly.

Aunt Karly turned one of the other black knobs to adjust the frequency. A tremendous racket filled the sitting room. Out of sheer nervousness, we laughed, and then we jumped when the static of the radio turned into a screaming voice. I couldn't understand much of it, except the shrieking about wiping out the *Belandas* – the Dutch – and the *Anjing Belandas* – the dogs of the Dutch, meaning the Indo-Europeans.

'Oh, do shut up!' shouted my aunt. 'I can't bear to listen to those angry young men with their horrible propaganda inciting hatred and murder. Bunch of brats!' Furiously, she turned the knobs.

I giggled.

'What are you laughing at now, Nell?' she said, annoyed.

'Brats sounds as though they're schoolboys.'

Aunt Karly didn't say anything, but I could see the trace of a smile on her lips. It made her look younger. She continued turning the knob until she had found the English frequency. Tensely, we listened to the English news. According to the report, today on 'Bloody Monday', lots of people had been rounded up in the streets. Hundreds of men and boys had been taken to the Simpang Club and there had been a bloodbath there. And it looked like the rest of the people who had been rounded up, had been taken to the Kalisosok prison. I hoped Tim was in the last group, but I didn't dare say so out loud. When the report had finished, the buzzing and crackling noise of the radio filled the sitting room again. We stayed there in front of the radio for a long time, in silence, staring at the illuminated glass panel, as if we were expecting to see the future light up like some crystal ball. Then my aunt switched off the radio. Suddenly she looked ten years older. Her head was bent, and her shoulders slumped.

'Can it get much worse than this?' I asked.

Aunt Karly took my hand, looking at me, but didn't know what to say.

For two weeks, I listened to the news on the radio with Aunt Karly several times a day. Sometimes I sat in front of it on my own, although my aunt preferred me not to. She thought the reports were too upsetting for me to listen to alone, but I took no notice. The radio was the only way to find out what was going on outside. Of course, I was afraid. More than I wanted to admit. If it wasn't safe anymore in Surabaya, I wanted to get away as soon as possible. We no longer dared to go out in the street and Aunt Karly had vetoed that anyway, saying: 'I'm not taking any risks. They're saying that most Indonesians now want an independent republic, and that the freedom fighters are prepared to do whatever it takes. So, we're better off staying home.'

'I can understand them wanting to be free, but I don't understand why they have no regard for the army or the police anymore.'

'I don't, either,' said Aunt Karly. 'I've also heard that Dutch people are being interned in the camps again and are being guarded by the Japanese. They say it's for their own safety.'

'I can't bear the thought of ending up in a camp with the Japs again.'

'You won't.'

'Dad had better find us soon or we'll have to get out of here.'

'And you're not to hang around outside unless it's absolutely necessary. Promise?'

'I'll stay in until it's safe enough for us to go out cycling together,' I said, to cheer her up but it didn't really work. She carried on fretting and I was still worried about Tim. I couldn't think of anything except what had gone on that day in the street; the way Tim had been thrown onto the truck with the other men and boys, the way he'd stood up, with his unruly mop of hair, his arms stretched out over the side, the way he fell down, and the way the truck had driven off with all those people inside it. My heart was pounding in my chest as I replayed those images again and again. Of course, as I had nothing to do all day, my thoughts kept going back to that late afternoon when Tim had been rounded up.

Time passed incredibly slowly. We heard on the radio that British troops had landed in the harbour here. That was two days ago. How far had they progressed now?

I was alone in the sitting room because Aunt Karly was taking a nap. I had set a chair by the table where the radio stood and turned the knob to find the right frequency for the English news. There was an appeal to the Dutch to come to the safe zones in Surabaya.

Camp 'De Wijk' in Darmo was named as a secure area. I crept ever closer to the speakers of the radio. I didn't want to miss a word of what was being said. English officers and soldiers would try to evacuate the people who had gathered in Darmo. I knew the secure area that they were talking about. It was a few streets away from the house where we were now living. Not far from where Lisa was. When we were evicted from our house in Surabaya by the Japs, my grandmother, my aunt, my mother and I had all been interned in camp 'De Wijk' for a few months before we were sent on to Ambarawa. Five, six families in one house. At the time, it had felt shabby and cramped, but I now knew that, compared to the Ambarawa camp, that had been a luxurious life.

The appeal on the radio was repeated one more time. I listened carefully and memorized all the details. This was a chance for us to get away from here. Perhaps I would see Tim again. Maybe he was out of prison and would also make his way to 'De Wijk'. I switched off the radio and ran upstairs. 'Auntie! Wake up! Wake up!'

Aunt Karly turned over and opened her eyes, reluctantly. 'Can't it wait, Nell? It can't be that urgent, can it?'

'Yes, it is, it's really important, otherwise I wouldn't disturb you. There's news. There's an appeal on the radio for us to leave.' I jumped up and down by her bed and could barely speak properly. I told her about the appeal to go to the secure area.

'They're taking everyone under protection to the harbour, to be evacuated to Singapore, because it's not safe here for Dutch people.'

Now my aunt was wide awake, sitting up straight in bed. 'Perhaps we should wait. To see if the reports are correct.'

'No, please let's go,' I begged. 'If it's true what they're saying on the radio, we have to try to get to that secure area as soon as possible.'

'But how do you know it's not a trap?'

'You don't know that,' I said. 'But if we leave now, we have the best chance of getting out.'

'And what about your father?' she asked.

'We've been waiting for him for so long. If it's so dangerous here, he probably can't get here, either. If my father's alive, he'll find us. Please, let's go!'

When my aunt was thinking, she had the habit of rubbing the sides of her nose with both hands. Then she made a decision and jumped out of bed, 'Alright, but we're not leaving here before I've heard the appeal on the radio myself. Then I might be able to really believe it.'

Our situation was precarious, of course, but I couldn't help being excited that finally something was about to happen. I was glad of our Bakelite radio. The big buzzing device with its black knobs was our salvation. How else would we have known we could leave here? Must leave here! Aunt Karly had now listened to the announcement and thought we should leave, because it really wasn't safe anymore, not even if we remained in hiding in the house. 'You're right, Nell,' she'd said to me. Yes, really! She agreed with me for once and she didn't do that lightly. Tonight, as soon as it was dark, we would leave for 'De Wijk'. Finally! We'd get away from here!

But although I was dying to leave, I was slow to pack. It took me ages to collect my things. First there was Tim's ring. I opened the little box holding the ring and stared at it for a long time. Then I took some black cord, that I had found in the sewing box and attached the ring to the cord, tied the cord with two firm knots, hung it around my neck and hid it under my blouse. Now I was sure I wouldn't ever lose it. I put the little box into the pocket of my skirt and folded the skirt.

When I folded my mother's coat, it was as if my mother were suddenly very close by and it felt as if I could touch her. In my mind, I could see our whitewashed villa with its big garden with oleanders, roses and *tjemaras*, the Indonesian firs that my father loved so much, because they brought shade into the garden and had their own particular scent. The house was not far from the airfield where my father worked. It was a on a dead-end street and our house was the last house at the end of it. I used to sit on a low wall beside the road, waiting until my father came driving home from his work as a pilot at the airfield. And as I sat waiting there, I always wondered where you would end up if the road had continued onwards past the paddy fields, on and on towards the end of everything. I could sharply remember how my mother, on the day of our departure from Jogja, had very quickly packed two suitcases and then made up a bundle of my things. Two suitcases and a *bungkusan*: we couldn't carry more than that. We had to leave behind all our furniture, the curtains, the carpets, the records, the record player, the radio, the books, the paintings, my paints and crayons, and my chessboard. Our house that had been so cosy and welcoming, and which had fitted us like a tailored coat, was left abandoned and lifeless. And the other thing we left behind that day, was the settled happy life of our little family, but I didn't know that at the time.

From the back seat of the car, I had watched our house receding for as long as possible and had tried to store every detail in my memory. The white walls, the small windows, the veranda and the low front wall where I used to sit waiting for my father. My mother didn't look back. She was looking at my father. She had put her arm around his shoulder and was sitting close to him as he drove. It was only now that I realized how difficult parting from him must have been for her. If only I could tell my mother how much I missed her. If only we could all go back together to that house with its lovely garden, back to that safe, carefree, life.

Stupid. I mustn't think of those things. It always made me cry and now it was so bad that I couldn't stop. I lay on the bed among the things that I had to pack and cried an ocean full of tears for my mother, whom I missed and who was never, ever coming back. For my father who was somewhere, maybe on his way, but who couldn't comfort me now, and for Tim, whom I might never see again. And finally, I cried for myself, for what had happened to me.

An hour later I was still lying on my bed. Night was falling. Aunt Karly was calling me. I got up and wrapped my things in the cloth and took everything to the sitting room. Auntie's rucksack was packed and waiting. I saw the light of the radio glowing in the twilight of the room, but there was no sound coming from the device. Aunt Karly was sitting in the semi-darkness by the radio and was turning the dials.

'It's not working anymore. Something wrong with the speakers, but it's served us well,' she said, as she switched the radio off. She looked at me for a moment. 'I found a map of the city in the cabinet here and I had a look to see where that safe area is, that they were talking about on the radio. It's a few streets away from here. I know exactly how to get there. As far as I'm concerned, we can go. What about you? Are you ready to leave? Packed everything, not forgotten anything? We won't be coming back here.'

I wanted to say something, but my vocal cords refused to work so I just nodded. Typical of my aunt, to be so well prepared. She got up, walked over to me, and held me tightly for a moment. Then she picked up her rucksack. 'Alright, we're off.'

We shut the door behind us, crossed the veranda to the gate, shut the gate behind us and then we were in the street. It was pretty dark. There were only a few lights on here and there. Auntie took my hand and together we crept as fast as we could past the houses in the street. It was more like running than creeping. My heart was racing. I was glad that, at last, we were doing something, but I was also scared. What would happen if we were to accidentally run into some *Pemudas*? Would they shoot us on the spot or spear us with their bamboo sticks? Overhead, I could hear the drone of an airplane. We both listened to it.

'The English,' whispered Auntie. And she pulled me into the dark recess of an abandoned school. Nobody could possibly see us there; it was too dark.

'Yes, the English,' I whispered back. 'It's a Dakota.'

'Of course, you'd know that. You're the daughter of a pilot, aren't you?'

We heard the Dakota flying in a northerly direction. We followed its dark shape with our eyes and saw white pamphlets come fluttering down from the little plane. One came down right by our hiding place in the shadows of the street.

I picked up the paper and read the message. The English were demanding that the *Pemudas* hand in their weapons before 30th October. I quickly calculated that they had three days left. I hoped the English would succeed in disarming the freedom fighters, then it would be much safer here. Aunt Karly pulled me onwards. 'We have to move on.' Quickly, we ran to the next block of houses. I had a stitch in my side but didn't dare say so. Auntie might stop for me, and then we might be arrested.

'It should be around here somewhere,' whispered Aunt Karly, softly. We crept on slowly in the dark until we came to a blockade with some soldiers. Aunt Karly turned to run away down one of the side-streets, but before she could do so, one of the soldiers called out:

'There are some refugees over there!'

'You're safe,' one of the other men said, reassuringly. An English officer took our luggage and led us to a house two streets further on. The house stood a little to the front of the other houses in the street, just like the house where Granny and Aunt Karly used to live, and where my mother and I had stayed, so I immediately took a liking to the place.

The English officer showed us to a room with a double bed. 'It might take a day or two before it's safe enough to take you to the port.'

I was hoping to leave immediately but when I turned to ask him why, he'd already gone, leaving Auntie's rucksack and my bundle on the floor. I flopped down onto the bed. 'Two days! Why so long?'

Aunt Karly came and lay down beside me. 'I know, Nell, every minute spent waiting is one too many for you. We've made it here in one piece! It could have been worse.'

'But now I'm stuck in a house again!' I sulked.

'Come on, Nelly. There are lots of people here. I don't think you'll be bored.'

I sat up immediately. 'Perhaps Lisa is here, too!'

WAITING

'Hello, Beauty, are you hungry?' asked a soldier. 'Help yourself.' He pointed to a table where food was laid out – rice, bananas, mangoes, chicken. When I saw the food, I realized for the first time how hungry I was, but I didn't dare to accept his invitation straight away. I smiled shyly at him and followed Aunt Karly through the lounge room, which was full of people. It was quite dark, because the windows had been blacked out and there was very little lighting. I counted four English soldiers and a group of people, who, just like us, had sought a safe place to stay: a girl of my age and three women. I could see that Lisa wasn't among them, and even though there'd only been a slim chance that she would be there, I was still disappointed. And of course, Tim certainly wasn't there. I hadn't expected him to turn up, but still, I had secretly hoped he might, against my better judgement.

We moved to a sofa in the corner of the room. 'I'm Karly and this is my niece, Nell,' said my aunt to a small group of people.

We shook hands with everyone, and they introduced themselves. I immediately forgot the names of the English soldiers. In their uniforms they all looked the same. The three women were the Deen sisters, and the girl was their niece. Aunt Karly didn't know them; they had been in a different camp to us. The girl was called Tina. Only when I shook her hand did I recognize her: Tina Scholten from Jogjakarta. In another life, I had often seen her at the swimming pool. A life with a mother, a father and a home.

'I almost didn't recognize you, Tina. It's been such a long time. I'm fifteen now and so are you, of course, but you've changed so much.'

Tina held my hand and laughed. 'So, have you. We were only little girls in Jogja and now look at us.'

I took another good look at her. I could hardly imagine that I had changed as much as Tina. She was very thin, but she looked like a young woman! I certainly didn't. Or did I?

Tina laughed at my surprised expression and when she did so, she reminded me of the girl I'd known so long ago. We went to the table and tentatively helped ourselves to a little chicken, rice and mango. As we held the plates in our hands, we looked at each other without saying anything. We knew that we were both thinking back to that time when we had hardly anything to eat at all. At the sight of all that food, we couldn't help ourselves, because the hunger from back then had been stored in our bodies.

'After seven years, every cell in your body has been replaced. That's why it will take at least seven years before we can think differently about food,' I said, and demonstratively I took a bite.

'It tastes wonderful,' said Tina, with her mouth full.

We ate the chicken and rice and never stopped talking. Soon, it felt as if we had seen each other only last week instead of almost four years ago. Tina told me that she had arrived at this house a few days ago. 'On the way here, I lost my mother.

I'm waiting for her, because I'm sure she's still alive, but as soon as there's another transfer to the harbour, I'm going. It's too dangerous to stay. Everyone says so.'

Tina didn't ask after my mother and I didn't want to mention her, either. Instead I said, 'I also lost someone. Perhaps you know him. He's called Tim. Tim Thissen, and on 14th October he was arrested in the streets of Surabaya and taken to prison. Perhaps you heard something about it and know where he is?'

'Tim Thissen? I don't know him, but I do know his mother and his sister! What a coincidence.'

'Really?' I could hardly believe it and felt hot and flustered. 'Tell me, what do you know?'

'Not much. I know that he was locked up, like you said. But then I heard that he's been released again.'

'And now? Where is he now?' I pressed her.

Tina shrugged her shoulders. 'No idea. With his mother, perhaps!'

I didn't feel particularly reassured by this but at least I knew he was out of prison. That was something. And he was alive. When I thought of that, I felt like singing out loud. Tim was alive!

One of the soldiers had found an accordion in a cupboard in the sitting room. It had ivory keys and a red Formica case. The soldier reminded me a bit of Tim. He had the same mouth. A cheerful mouth that curled up at the corners. The soldier strapped on the instrument and played us a few songs. It made the sitting room seem bright and cheerful. It felt a little strange, all that unaccustomed light-heartedness. Outside, the *Pemudas* were carrying on their fight for independence, and inside we were waiting for a safe moment to be taken to the harbour to be evacuated by ship. The soldier had a rough voice and he was clearly enjoying playing. He sang a few jolly

English dance songs, making it almost impossible to stay in your chair. Tina and I danced around the room. We felt carefree and happy until the accordion player started singing a German song and the dancing stopped abruptly.

We stood in a corner of the room and listened to his rendition of Kurt Weill's song *Surabaya Johnny*, about a girl whose heart had been broken by a sailor who had abandoned her. My father loved that song. He used to keep playing that record until my mother couldn't bear it anymore and they started arguing. 'Why don't you play something else? I can't stand that Lotte Lenya anymore,' she cried. 'It's too melancholy and it always makes me homesick.'

Usually, my father took no notice and carried on playing the record anyway.

'I love you more than Lenya loves her sailor,' my mother would shout, and then she'd sing along: *Surabaya Johnny. Mein Gott und ich liebe dich so. Surabaya Johnny. Warum bin ich nicht froh?* It was strange to hear that English soldier singing that German song: *Surabaya Johnny. My God I love you so. Surabaya Johnny, why don't I feel joy?* Now I was the one who was feeling sad, just like my mother used to.

'That's a sad song,' said Tina. 'German is a beautiful language, what a pity that the war has made it so ugly.'

'My mother hated that song. Now she's dead.'

'I guessed so. I'm so sorry.'

'Yes, she died one-hundred and eighty-three days ago in the camp. And now, sometimes I wake up and I can't remember what her face looked like and then I get into a panic because I don't want to forget anything about her.' I swallowed and wiped my tears away with my hand. 'And then I want to be with her even though I know that will never be possible again.'

Tina put her arm around me. 'Of course, you miss her, especially now. You had a lovely mother.'

I nodded. 'And I miss my father, too, and I don't know where he is. And I think about Tim, but I don't know if I'll ever see him again, either.'

'You're going to find your father and Tim again. I'm sure of that.'

I stayed silent. How could Tina know any of that for sure? Where did she find those certainties when every minute things were changing all around us? 'Wishful thinking,' my father would have said. He hated it. I put my hand on top of Tina's, which was resting on my upper arm, and watched the soldier take off the accordion and go back outside to the guard post. The silence he left behind him, filled the room.

Aunt Karly came over to us. She had been talking to the Deen sisters all evening. 'Are you coming, Nell? I think it's time we went to sleep.'

'Good idea,' I answered, hoping that she couldn't tell that I'd been crying. 'See you tomorrow, Tina.'

'See you tomorrow, Nell, and sleep well.'

Deeper, I had to dig down deeper and faster. Much faster. Our safe house was completely covered with earth and we had to dig ourselves out before the *Pemudas* came back. There seemed to be no end to it. There was still so much earth that we had to dig out before the tunnel would be long enough to escape. I had to keep working. *Keep digging. Mustn't stop.* I was suddenly woken up by a crash as if something fell over in the room and I sat up.

'Look out. Keep digging, I'm not ready yet, I have to do more digging before they come back.'

'Nelly, you're dreaming,' said Auntie. 'We're safe here.

I knocked over a chair, that's all.'

I looked at her sleepily. 'When do we leave for the harbour?'

'It's still early... get some more sleep. I'm going downstairs to see what they're up to.'

I mumbled something and when the door closed softly behind her, I dropped back on my pillow. I stretched out a couple of times and tried to shake off the bad dream by imagining that I was floating on water and doing the backstroke. Stroke, stroke, kick. What a night. I'd never slept so badly. I wasn't used to lying next to Aunt Karly anymore. Funny how fast I'd lost the habit once I had my own bed again. Stroke, stroke, kick. A day or two, the soldier had said, but I was sure we would be leaving today and not tomorrow.

I leapt out of bed and stood in front of the big mahogany wardrobe. Sleepily, I looked in the big mirror on its door. What could be stored in such a big wardrobe? I was so curious that I couldn't resist opening the door. Dresses! It was full of dresses. Intrigued, I moved some of the hangers and looked at a few of them. Most of them were boring, but one dress made of white satin stood out. It had really pretty red and green ribbons along the sleeves and I couldn't stop myself from taking the dress out of the wardrobe and trying it on to see how it looked on me. I turned a pirouette in front of the mirror. Yes, it was beautiful. If only Tim could see me like this! That thought made me dizzy.

'We can take our time,' said Aunt Karly, as she came into the room. 'There's no rush. We're not leaving today.'

'We're not?' I asked, disappointed. 'Why not?'

'No idea. Apparently, it's not safe at the moment and anyway, you can't go anywhere dressed like that,' answered my Aunt, as she pointed at my outfit.

'Why not?' I asked, surprised.

'A white dress is not very practical for a trip in a truck to the harbour, is it? But it does look good on you!'

Embarrassed, I smoothed the skirt. I was so stunned by Auntie's news that our departure had been delayed, that I had forgotten that I was wearing a dress that wasn't mine. 'I was curious, so I looked in the wardrobe.'

'And you found *that*,' said my aunt with a laugh. 'It's gorgeous and it really suits you. Take it with you.'

'I can't do that, can I? It belongs to someone else, doesn't it?'

'Well, it used to belong to somebody…'

'The person who lived in this house?'

'Maybe, or to someone who, just like us, stayed here for a while and was evacuated. I don't think it really belongs to anyone, now.'

'So, can I take it with me?' I asked blankly. I could hardly believe it.

'Do you want to take it with you?'

'Oh yes, of course!'

'Well, that's settled then,' said Aunt Karly, with satisfaction. 'Now we just have to get out of here! I've asked the English soldiers to inform the Red Cross that we're being evacuated to Singapore. They said they had already done that so your father will still be able to find us.'

'Perhaps he's already there!' I said, merrily, 'and then we'll see him soon.'

'And I'll see you again in a minute. I'm just going to talk to the Deen sisters.'

When my aunt had left, I turned another pirouette in the white dress in front of the mirror. Would Tim like the dress? Tim! I had to let him know that I wouldn't be in Surabaya anymore. In the cupboard, I found notepaper, and with shaking fingers I wrote:

'Dear Tim,

Tomorrow, 29th October, I'll be leaving for Singapore with my aunt on an English ship. My father is probably there.

I really hope you found your mother. Then one day you can give her the ring you showed me on the train. You lost that ring and I found it for you.

See you in Singapore.'

I didn't write: 'I'm not sure if we're leaving tomorrow', or 'I really hope to see you again.' That would be tempting fate. I'd definitely never see him again if I did that. And without thinking, I wrote *love Nelly* at the bottom of the letter and put the letter into an envelope. Then I thought about the word *love*, that was floating somewhere across the paper, and I blushed bright red, but there was nothing to be done about it. The envelope had already been sealed.

I took off the white dress and put on my old skirt. I folded the dress up and put it in my *bungkusan* on top of my mother's coat. I planted a kiss on the envelope and put that on top of the dress. Later on, I would give it to one of the soldiers to deliver to the Red Cross. Another whole day to go, but tomorrow we'd be leaving! I ran out of the room and went looking for Tina.

The next morning, the soldiers still weren't getting ready for the evacuation. The army trucks that were supposed to pick us up were nowhere to be seen. More women had arrived at the house and the atmosphere was grim. Were we supposed to wait until there was a certain number of evacuees? Nobody knew. I was too restless to sit still, so I went back and forth between the bedroom and the sitting room in the hope of finding out more.

'I want to get away from here,' complained Tina. 'I want to go and look for my mother. I've been here for several days already. If it takes any longer, I'm afraid I'll lose my mother forever.'

'They promised me and Aunt Karly that we would leave today', I said. 'I heard the soldiers talking this morning. They were saying something happened yesterday, but no-one wants to talk about it. I've asked everyone, but I'm not getting any answers.'

'Perhaps they know more outside!'

Together, Tina and I went up to the soldiers who were standing at the guard post in front of the house.

'You're not allowed to come out here,' grumbled the accordion player. His usual smile had disappeared; his face was tight and stern.

'What's going on? Why won't anyone tell us anything? Aren't we safe here? Is that it?' asked Tina. 'If something's happened, then shouldn't we leave for the harbour immediately?' She smiled at the soldier. His face didn't change. He wasn't going to answer any of her questions and gestured that we should make ourselves scarce. 'It's not safe out here.'

That morning, life seemed to have ground to a halt. Nothing happened. But then at noon, we all had to get ready for departure. And then we carried on waiting. Late afternoon, I discovered that there were several large army trucks parked out in the street.

'Yes. We're really leaving today!' I was so excited, I couldn't stand still, and hopped from one foot to the other.

'Let's wait and see, Nelly, but it does look like it,' said Aunt Karly.

'Of course, we're leaving! And it's about time, too. This is the second day! And it won't be long before we leave because soon it will be dark.' Impatiently, I pointed at the large army trucks parked in the street. 'That really looks like we're going. Why else would I be standing out here at the guard post with you and everybody else from the house? I'm not standing here for nothing, am I? I've got everything I want to take right here.'

'Let's wait and see,' repeated Auntie, quietly.

I couldn't understand how she could stay so calm. I was bursting with energy. And I was hot, not just from excitement about the forthcoming departure, but mostly because of what I was wearing. There was hardly any space for luggage on the truck and I didn't want to leave my mother's coat behind, so I had put it on. Auntie predicted that I would be far too hot, but I still wore it. It was the only way I could take the coat with me. So now I was boiling hot, but I was pretending for Auntie that I wasn't.

More and more people from the other houses had poured into the street and they had gathered around the first of the trucks. I looked at the loading space with the high sides. Would all those people really fit in that truck? I looked at the English soldiers. They held their weapons at the ready, their movements disciplined, and their faces were tense and focused. I nudged Aunt Karly. 'The soldiers are getting ready!'

Auntie nodded and gently squeezed my arm. She wanted to say something, but at that moment there was a stirring in the group.

'Move on,' called the English soldiers and they gestured that we had to get in. Mothers with children first and then the other women. The evacuees from our house were the last to clamber on. Tina and the Deen sisters were in another truck because I couldn't see them anywhere. Auntie and I were the last to get on.

'Stay flat on the floor of the truck,' yelled the soldier who had played the accordion, as he shut the tailgate. 'You have to make yourselves invisible. Understood? Invisible!'

Could the soldier explain how you did that, make yourself invisible? The driver started the engine and the people rolled around in the back until the truck had picked up speed. No-one said anything. I lay beside my aunt on the floor of the truck and looked at the dusky sky above us. I tried to get my bearings by watching the treetops that whizzed by, and the top of an occasional building. Now and then I heard a small child crying and listened to its mother trying to soothe and quieten it. I listened to the engine of the truck. As long as we were moving, we were safe. If we were to stop and someone were to look in the back, we would no longer be invisible. Then we would be lost.

It got hotter and hotter in the truck. No wonder, with all those warm bodies pressed together. Sweat trickled down my forehead, neck, back and calves. Perhaps I should have lain on top of the coat instead of putting it on, but I was worried the soldiers wouldn't have allowed it. Now I was incredibly hot. I was almost melting.

The wool of the coat tickled my skin. My father had given my mother that coat when the three of us were on holiday in America. We had driven from St Louis to San Francisco.

In the daytime, it was almost as hot there as it was here in the truck. *Don't think about that, it will only make you feel even hotter.* In the evenings, it had cooled down. We had driven through the Grand Canyon, Santa Fe, Boulder City, Death Valley, Sacramento and on towards San Francisco. Every evening, my father drove on for far too long, and every evening he got into an argument with my mother about when to stop. Then, to make up, and to smooth over all the arguments, my father had bought my mother that coat. A handwoven woollen coat, with Indian patterns embroidered in earthy colours. A coat like a landscape. I had sat in the back of the car and, half-asleep, had listened to the engine and to my parents' voices. Just like I was now listening to the engine of the truck.

Why had my father returned to Indonesia? Why did he take us to the war? Why didn't he stay in America? Where was he now? These questions rose up and repeated themselves each time the hurtling truck thundered through a pothole.

I was on my way to the port of Surabaya, on my way to safety. A breeze carried the smell of the sea into the truck. The port couldn't be far off now. Suddenly, the truck stopped. The people in the truck came alive again. 'Where are we?' I felt a cool sea breeze. Auntie said we could get out. I sat up, and the wind picked me up and carried me to a place where all was quiet. So quiet. Where was my father?

TO SINGAPORE

Just as unexpectedly as it had come, the stillness had disappeared again. Far away and very softly, I heard a ship's horn, cars, people. I was lying stretched out on something soft and warm and all I could see were legs. I was surrounded by a waving forest of ankles, calves and knees, and somewhere in the middle, Aunt Karly was crouching down beside me. She was holding my hand.

'She's coming round,' said a strange voice. Two brown eyes looked searchingly at me. A mouth with curling corners. For a moment I thought it was Tim, but it was the accordion soldier. I smiled at him weakly. The soldier gestured to the onlookers to walk on. 'Move on, everyone, move on.'

The forest around me started moving and I wanted to sit up, but the soldier pushed me down gently. 'Take your time.' He gave me some water from a field bottle.

Aunt Karly squeezed my hand to reassure me. 'You fainted.'

'I just remember getting hotter and hotter.'

'You were overheated, and when you stood up in the truck, you fainted. We took off your coat, so you could cool down and laid you here on the quay.'

I smiled vaguely. It was sweet of Auntie, not to mention that she had told me not to wear that coat because it would be much too hot. I wanted to ask where the coat was, but then I realized I was lying on top of it. 'It smells nice here, of the sea and boats,' I said.

'And oil,' added Aunt Karly.

'And tar.'

'Rust.'

'Fish.'

'Sweat! You smell like an otter. I'm glad you're getting talkative again, and I can see some colour returning to your cheeks.' Auntie pointed to a spot a few hundred metres further along the quayside, where people were running back and forth in the dusk. 'Do you think you can get up slowly, so we can join the queue for boarding?'

'Well, I can't lie here forever, can I? They might leave without us.' I got up, groggily. The quayside swayed back and forth, and I held on to my *bungkusan* like a lifebelt. I had to wait for the dizziness to pass.

'Are you alright?' asked Aunt Karly. I could hear the concern in her voice, so I gave her my 'there's nothing to worry about' smile. I didn't want to wait any longer! I wanted to board that ship. Auntie picked up the coat and together we walked on.

The accordion soldier stood at the gangway to the ship. 'Take care, shorty!' He smiled at me, tapping his cap with two fingers, and then he strode across the quay to the other soldiers of his unit.

'What does he mean by "shorty"?' I said indignantly. 'I'm not short at all!'

'Your English isn't bad at all,' said Auntie.

'Well, I can understand it, because my mother used to talk to me in English.' I had never answered my mother in English, and I don't know why.

The sailors on the ship gestured that we should come on board. The ship that would take us to Singapore was moored on the outside of a row of four ships. As we boarded the first ship, lights started coming on in the other ships along the quay. It all looked very festive. Surely that was a good sign. With the help of the sailors, we clambered from the rear of one ship to the next, from deck to deck. Take a stride. Jump and another big stride. Auntie was concerned about me, worried that I would faint again, but I was enjoying myself and cried: 'At last things are happening.' Excitedly, I jumped onto the deck of the third ship.

'You're probably right,' said Aunt Karly, 'For you, just being on the road is more important than the destination, but I'm glad we've got here.' Visibly relieved, Aunt Karly stepped aboard the final ship, the *Ekma*. It was a two-deck schooner of the British-Indian steam company that was now being deployed for troop transport. It was like stepping into another world. The lights were on and the sailors in their smart white uniforms were cheerful and they clapped their hands as we boarded. Some whistled on their fingers, too. It gave me butterflies in my tummy. This world was such a merry place. Big, clean and well-organized. You could walk around the ship without being afraid that you would run into a group of *Pemudas* or anything else that made your blood run cold. It felt wonderfully safe.

'This is your cabin,' said the sailor, who led the way across the teak upper deck of the ship. He pointed at an open door and disappeared. I followed Auntie into the cabin. It was a small room with two bunkbeds. There were two women sitting on one of the bottom bunks. It took me a while to realize that it was Tina, who was sitting there with Mrs Deen, one of her three aunts.

Before I could say anything, Tina sprang up and hugged me. 'Are you alright, Nell? I was so frightened when I saw you lying stretched out on the quay. I was afraid we'd have to leave without you.'

'No way!' I pushed Tina away from me to have a good look at her. 'I just can't believe it. After years, I meet you in the safe house and now I'm sharing the same cabin with you. What a coincidence.'

'There's no such thing as coincidence, Nelly. We're just meant to be together on this ship, and look, here you are!'

'Yes, here I am,' I agreed. I threw my bundle onto one of the top bunk beds and laid my mother's coat beside it. 'And I'm safe! At last.'

'Well, relatively safe,' said Tina. 'There's a chance that the ship will hit a mine at sea. The Java Sea is full of them.'

Stunned, I looked at her. Was she trying to scare me on purpose?

'I'm not making that up, you know.'

'Not much chance of that happening,' said Aunt Karly, in a tone that ruled out contradiction, but she looked a little pale. She shook Tina's hand first, and then Mrs Deen's. 'I'm glad we're sharing a cabin with you. And there's even a porthole with a view of the sea. Not bad!'

'All the sailors have given up their cabins for the evacuees. They're sleeping on deck,' said Mrs Deen.

'How very kind of them,' answered Aunt Karly.

I hopped from one foot to the other. I would have preferred to sleep outside, too, watching the stars in a jet-black sky, and listening to the sea. I wanted to get out of there. Out of the cabin. To experience something else. I really wanted to explore the ship with Tina. It was much too cramped and small inside the cabin. 'Can Tina and I go and have a look around the deck?'

'As long as you don't do anything silly and come and tell us where you're hanging out, that's fine by me,' answered Auntie.

'Okay, I will!' I gave her a kiss and walked to the door.

Grinning, Tina came and stood next to me. 'We'll let you know where we are, so that you'll know which way Nelly will be swimming when we hit a mine. I'll take good care of her if that happens!'

'I'm not anticipating any problems with mines,' said Auntie, 'but it won't hurt to look after Nell anyway. The more guardian angels one has these days, the better.'

It was pleasantly cool out on deck and it was wonderful to be out of that stuffy little cabin. I soon felt a lot more cheerful as I stood with Tina at the back of the ship and leant against the railing. From the upper deck, we looked out at Oedjoeng, the naval base of Surabaya. The dust had settled over the harbour. There were hardly any people walking on the quayside now, and only an occasional car drove by. Except for a few small lights on the ships, it was dark.

'I've never been here before. What about you?' asked Tina.

'Me neither. The times I boarded a ship with my mother and father, we left from Tandjoengperak, the harbour for passenger ships further on.'

'I've been there to pick someone up from the boat once or twice, but I've never been on one myself before!'

'Really?' I couldn't imagine anyone never having travelled on a ship before. I thought of my trip to America with my father and mother.

'No, honestly. This is my first sea voyage and there's bound to be a storm at sea.'

'Aren't you the optimist,' I joked. 'Storms at sea, ships hitting mines and disasters in Surabaya, instead of just travelling to Singapore!'

'That's what you hope, but you never know for sure if you'll end up where you want to go.'

I was silent. I knew Tina had lost her mother on their way to the safe house, but I didn't know what I should say about that.

A group of sailors walked by. One of the sailors turned round and smiled at me in a friendly way: 'Yes! Singapore, Madame, Singapore, God willing.' He winked at me and without saying anything more, he walked on with the rest. I watched them until they had gone and said, triumphantly, 'Well, there you are. If that sailor says we're going to Singapore, then that's what will happen!'

'That sailor was flirting with you, Nell! You can't take him seriously.'

'No way! He was just being friendly, and anyway, why should he flirt with me? I'm only fifteen. Well, almost sixteen.'

'That's what you call flirting!' Tina insisted.

I shrugged my shoulders. I didn't know that being cheerful was the same as flirting, but Tina seemed to know what she was talking about. Anyway, I shouldn't listen to her. I wanted to believe the sailor. We were going to Singapore. That was closer to Japan than Surabaya. The ship would take me closer to my father, because he was surely also on his way to Singapore. That thought made me feel really happy. And Tim would surface somewhere, too.

Suddenly I realized that I had forgotten to give my letter to Tim to a soldier at the safe house! *Oh, how stupid!* I went hot all over. Now Tim wouldn't know where I was. He didn't even know I was on board this ship. If I were to leave now, I would be getting closer to my father, but I would probably never see Tim again! I couldn't remember what I had done with the letter. Was it still in my *bungkusan*? In that case, I had to somehow get that letter delivered to the Red Cross.

'What's up?' asked Tina.

'Nothing. Let's go back to the cabin,' I suggested.

'So soon? Is something the matter?'

'No, but I want to write to my father that I've boarded the ship to Singapore. And then I've got to see if I can get that letter delivered to a Red Cross post here in Surabaya.'

'So that they know you're in the Java Sea when we sink?'

I glared at Tina but said nothing.

'Joke, Nelly. It was just a joke,' said Tina. 'I'm guessing that you want to let Tim know where you are.'

I felt myself blushing and wanted to say something, but Tina rambled on and I gave up.

'There's notepaper in the cabin. Enough to write him ten letters. Go on.'

'See you later,' I called. I didn't tell her I had already written the letter before we left for the harbour. Before Tina could say anymore, I ran back to our cabin. There was no-one there. My fingers were trembling as I took my bundle from the bed and searched for the letter. I found it at the bottom. Thank goodness! With the envelope in my hand I ran back to the rear of the ship. That letter had to be delivered as quickly as possible. I searched the deck, but I couldn't see anyone to ask to deliver my post. That was something I hadn't counted on. Resolutely, I climbed over the railing, just as I had done a few hours before, but then in the other direction, and I stepped onto the deck of the neighbouring ship. I went from deck to deck again. Stride. Jump and then another big stride. Without a sailor beside you to lend you a helpful hand, as on the way there, it was a lot harder. But a few minutes later, I jumped onto the quay, which was now completely dark and deserted. There wasn't a sailor to be seen. I bit my lip and tears stung my eyes. Suddenly, someone grabbed hold of me, and I felt the iron grip of a hand on my shoulder. I was so scared that I couldn't breathe, as if that hand were choking me.

'What the hell are you doing here?' hissed a man's voice, furiously.

I waved the envelope and hoped he would understand that that letter needed posting, but it only made him more furious.

'Speak up, girl, does your mother know you are out here?' he asked, angrily.

'No, she died!' I shouted back. 'And this needs to be posted to the Red Cross.'

He let go of me. 'Good Lord,' sighed the man, and he introduced himself as officer David Jones. He looked at me in a much more friendly way. And although I had never wanted to speak English with my mother, I heard myself explaining in fluent English why I was standing on the quay with a letter to Tim. That I was afraid, that otherwise I would never see him again. I didn't know I had so much English stored up, but now that I had got myself into trouble, it all came pouring out. Where had those words been hiding all that time?

'Okay, I'll deliver the letter and I'll make enquiries about Tim, too,' promised officer David Jones. He put the envelope into his trouser pocket. 'If I find out anything about him, I'll make sure that information reaches you in Singapore. But now, you'd better get back to your ship,' and he escorted me back to the T.S.S. *Ekma*.

Stride. Jump and another big stride, I was getting better at it. As soon as I stepped onto the deck of the fourth ship, he disappeared back ashore, without saying goodbye.

I was walking across the deck, back to the cabin but stopped when I heard Aunt Karly's voice. She was standing next to the lifeboats and talking to the captain. I wanted to slip by, but she caught sight of me.

'Where did you just appear from?' she asked, annoyed. 'I was looking for you and couldn't find you anywhere. Tina didn't know where you were, either. You said you would come and tell me if you were leaving the top deck and going elsewhere on the ship! I need to know where you are, Nell. You went off on another adventure on your own, didn't you?'

'I was just on the first deck.' It was the first time in my life that I had lied to Aunt Karly, but it didn't seem like a good time to tell her that I had been to the quayside on my own. For the rest of the journey, she would be worried to death about me.

'You mustn't lie to me, Nell. I don't know what you've been up to, but you were not on the first deck, that's for sure.'

'That was a lovely evening.' I took a sip of my Earl Grey tea. Now that I was sitting up in bed, I could feel the way the ship heaved much more strongly. We had departed at ten o'clock at night. The captain had ordered everyone to stay inside until we had reached open water. There had been music in the ship's lounge and even dancing. Some of the girls had danced with the sailors. I hadn't dared to, but it was nice that there was music.

'My head is full of all those catchy songs. I haven't felt this light and jolly in years.'

'You're like a balloon that's slipped free and is now floating high in the sky,' said Aunt Karly, from the bunk below me.

'Well, it's the first time since we left Ambarawa, that I feel free. And such luxury! I'm lying between clean sheets with a cup of tea. This must be it. This is it!'

'This is what?' asked Auntie Karly. 'What do you mean? Not that this is Singapore? We won't be there for a long time, yet.'

'No, I know. But I mean: this is it! This is the moment of ultimate freedom! Can't you feel it, Auntie? This moment here, this tea, the lights we can see in the distance on the shore, the English that is being spoken. It's all part of the freedom of this moment. Freedom that you can hear, see, smell and taste.'

'If I didn't know better, I would think you'd been drinking,' said Aunt Karly, laughing.

'Drunk on freedom perhaps. It's like being back on the *Clipfontein* with my mother again. That was before the war, when we were on our way back from San Francisco to Surabaya. That was a really fun, luxurious voyage. My mother danced the whole way.'

'Yes, that's true,' answered Auntie, 'I remember that very well. March 1941. With Gran, I picked you up from the ship and the first thing you said was, that your mother could dance so beautifully.'

'Did I say that? I don't remember, but it was true. The whole voyage, I watched my mother dancing and after a while I'd seen her swirling around the room so often that it was as if it were me who was out there on the dance floor.'

That first night on the ship, I dreamt of the *Clipfontein*. I was dancing in the lounge with Aunt Karly, as my mother danced a waltz with the captain, faster and faster. They spun around until with a final swish, they flew over the railing and disappeared into the sea. I shouted out but no-one heard me. The people around me just carried on dancing.

I woke up sweating from my nightmare and looked out through the port-hole at the stars. I listened to the throbbing of the ship's engine as the ship swayed along to the rhythm of the sea. It was very hot. My bed was narrow. But the clean sheets were nice. No-one was asleep; everyone was pretending they were. I knew for certain that I would never be a sailor when I grew up. When life was back to normal again, I never again wanted to sleep in such a cramped space with lots of other people around me. It reminded me of life in the Ambarawa camp. *Don't think about that.* It made me much too sad. *Think of something else.* I pictured Tim looking at the stars somewhere, just like we had done together on the train to Surabaya when we had first met each other. I didn't want to think of anything else. Couldn't think of anything else. I thought of how I would wrap my arms around him and how I would kiss him. No, I would never dare do that. He would know immediately that I had never kissed anyone before.

Aunt Karly had heard that I was awake and was standing next to my bed. 'I can't sleep, either. Luckily, it's only two days' sailing and then we'll be in Singapore. I just hope your father is there, too. Perhaps he left Japan for Manila in the Philippines, and he can travel from there to Singapore.'

I sat up. 'I wish my father would hurry up and find me. Why is it taking so long? Why have I lost everyone I care about? My mother, my father, Tim…?'

Aunt Karly stroked my hair. 'You still have me.'

I felt ashamed. I put my hand on my aunt's. 'Of course,

I still have you. And now that my mother's gone, we belong together even more.'

Aunt Karly gave me a kiss. 'Don't worry. You'll find your father. I know that for sure. And now let's get some sleep.' Auntie returned to her own bed. I listened to her breathing and stared straight ahead into the darkness. I touched the ring that hung by a cord around my neck.

Did Tim belong with me? I hardly knew him. But still. Yes, it felt as if Tim was a part of me. He was the first person to have made me laugh again since the camp, to make me feel alive again. I wanted to see him again more than my own father. I promised myself that I'd carry on wearing his ring on a cord around my neck until I found him!

WHERE IS EVERYONE?

'Camp Wilhelmina – you'd think a refugee camp in Singapore with such a strange name would amount to something,' I grumbled, as I walked out of the camp office with my aunt. It was a big camp with a central canteen and administration office, and tidy rows of small stone houses. The heat was oppressive, and I was feeling cross because our enquiries about my father and Tim had so far led to nothing. 'Camp Wilhelmina is full of Dutch people who have lost each other,' I moaned.

Aunt Karly tried to say something, but I wasn't listening and ranted on. 'The Red Cross does nothing but compile new lists of survivors. I've stopped believing they can actually reunite anyone. My father still hasn't located us. On the ship, someone said that Singapore is called *Pulau Ujong* in Malaysian.'

Aunt Karly was glad she could interrupt my tirade. '*Pulau Ujong* means "island at the end".'

'Exactly, yes! And that's where we are: at the end of the world, where no-one will ever find us again.'

'Don't be ridiculous. The camp is fine.'

'Yes, I know! We survived, that is much more important.

I agree! But it's also hot, dusty and most of all, incredibly boring.'

'Stop moaning, Nell! We've only been here two days!' chided my aunt. She hated my rants.

'On board the *Ekma*, I couldn't wait to get to Singapore, and now I wish I were back on board the ship.'

'Perhaps you can sail back with them!'

For a moment, I thought she was serious, but then she grinned and together we started laughing.

'I'm sorry, Auntie. You don't deserve to be moaned at like that. But doesn't it bother you at all, the way things are here?'

'I don't concern myself with that too much, Nell. I spend more time thinking about what I want to do once I get away from here. Where I want to go afterwards.'

'Where you want to go? You're here with me, aren't you?' I asked, and I stopped in the middle of the dusty path. I felt the heat and panic rising up inside me.

Aunt Karly put her hand on my shoulder. 'I'm not going to leave you here on your own, Nell. You don't have to worry about that. But I will have to start living my own life again when things get back to normal. I used to think I would share my life with Chris, but he got shot, and didn't survive the war, so the life I dreamed of is no longer possible.'

'What will you do?' Slowly, we walked on. I looked at her from aside. I couldn't imagine a life without Aunt Karly. Ever since we'd been imprisoned in Ambarawa more than three years ago, we had been together every single day. 'Do you have any plans?'

'I'm thinking about going to Holland. To visit Chris's family.'

'But you don't know them!'

'That's true, but it's a chance to start over. Don't worry. I'll stay with you. I won't leave you on your own. If I do go to Holland, it will be both of us together.'

I shrugged my shoulders and didn't reply. I didn't want Auntie Karly to go to Holland. It was upsetting, that she wanted to go there, but I didn't feel like discussing it with her now. I preferred to go and see if I could find Lisa. She always cheered me up.

'I'm going to see Lisa. Is that alright? I'll see you in a bit.'

'Lisa? Is she here too? I didn't know that.'

'I met her yesterday by chance. She got here three days before us.'

'And you keep saying there's nothing to do here! Say hello to Lisa for me. I'll see you later.' Aunt Karly waved and walked on. I took a left turn to the western part of the camp.

Lisa was sitting outside the little stone house where she and her aunts and cousins had been quartered. She looked pale as a ghost and didn't react when I went and stood right in front of her. Silently, I sat down beside her. After a long time, Lisa started talking. 'Only the youngest brother and Trudy survived the shooting. The rest are dead.'

At first, I didn't know what she was talking about, but as she continued, it slowly became clear.

'I just found out what happened, and I'm devastated. One of my cousins heard the news and came to tell us. I just can't believe it. Something horrible happened on one of the trips with the army trucks. You know, those trucks which took us to the docks before we sailed to Singapore. On 28th October, one of them was ambushed.'

My heart started beating faster. 'Where?'

'Right on the corner of the Embong Sonokembang and South Palmen Street. They say that the trucks were shot at for hours. Many people were wounded, and they think that at least a hundred women and children died.'

'28th October was the day we were made to wait outside before leaving the safe house. I knew something was wrong that day!'

'Just the youngest boy and Trudy survived the shooting. The rest of the De Wit family are dead. Trudy, our Trudy, is in hospital in Singapore with a bullet wound in her arm. Her family is dead.'

'Her mother, too?'

'Her mother, and her twin sister, Jo. They're all dead. They were being evacuated from Goebeng to a safer place and the truck they were in was ambushed by freedom fighters. Hardly anyone survived.'

I listened to her and felt helpless. 'And what about their father? Is he still alive?'

'Dead, too. He'd already been taken away,' whispered Lisa.

I felt sick. I wanted to speak but didn't know what to say. The truck carrying my aunt and me had arrived safely. We hadn't been ambushed and were still alive. For once, we had been lucky. But it was stupid to say so.

'The Japs have been beaten and there's supposed to be peace!' said Lisa, as tears streamed down her face. 'So why is everyone still fighting?'

I took Lisa's hand and moved closer to her. For a long while we sat close together on the little veranda, holding hands. Without saying anything, we knew that we were both thinking of our last visit to the newly reunited De Wit family in their cheerful home in Surabaya. We'd been so jealous, Lisa and me. They had their family back, and we didn't. Now we were ashamed of our jealousy. There was almost no-one left of that happy family. We were alive, and they weren't.

'Just an hour ago, I was complaining to Auntie Karly, that it's all so boring here,' I said, to break the silence.

'Just like you!'

'Well, it is boring here, but from now on, I'm not going to moan anymore.'

'Never again?'

'I mean it, Lisa! Really never again.' I resolved not to complain if Auntie Karly decided to go to the Netherlands. I would just go with her.

That night, I dreamt I was walking on my own through a completely deserted Camp Wilhelmina. It was dead quiet. Everyone had left while I was sleeping, and no-one had warned me. In the distance, I could hear a car and not long after, without slowing down, my father tore by in his Ford with my mother and Auntie Karly beside him. He beeped his horn and drove past me at full speed. He hadn't recognized me. I felt totally abandoned. I woke up crying. Where was my father? And why couldn't anyone tell me where Tim was? *Ssh, mustn't think like that.* It was just a dream.

SO HERE I AM

'Your father is on his way,' said the lady at the Red Cross office. 'You must keep on believing he will come. Be glad you still have a father.'

I wanted to scream that I would be the judge of whether I was happy with that or not. Just in time, I bit my tongue. I wasn't going to complain anymore. Instead, I said: 'You're right, ma'am. A lost father is still a father.' Then I took a deep breath and walked out of the office.

Today, was Monday, November 12th. Leon Trotsky had been expelled from the Communist Party exactly 18 years ago on November 12th, 1927 to make way for Stalin. Which proved, that there was something wrong with that date. I wondered why I had remembered this odd fact from the history lessons at school. But if my father was coming, it certainly wouldn't be today.

I had been in Camp Wilhelmina for six days by then. Every morning, I enquired after my father at the Red Cross, just like I'd done for almost three months while I'd been in Surabaya. Since the arrival of his letter with the news that he was still alive, I hadn't heard a word from him. Maybe he was dead or maybe he wasn't bothered about seeing me anymore.

For whatever reason, he was taking a ridiculously long time to get here.

'The war has turned the whole world upside down. Travelling and sending information takes much longer than it used to,' Auntie had said, just that morning. 'Try and be patient.'

'But I'm not!'

'Just try a little harder, Nell.'

'Why doesn't Dad try harder!' It was stupid to argue with my aunt again. I hadn't meant to. I didn't want to constantly be a nuisance because she was really doing her best for me. That's why I'd gone by myself to enquire at the office for any news. I'd hoped that Singapore would bring me closer to my father, but he was just as absent as ever. I decided I wasn't going to wait for him any longer. I was past caring.

Deep in thought, I sauntered across the big open space of the camp. Now and then, I kicked at a stone. I didn't want to go back to Aunt Karly. I wished I could make plans, just like her, for what I wanted to do with my life once we were able to leave Camp Wilhelmina. What would I do if it were all up to me? I didn't have a clue. What was Lisa going to do? Perhaps we could go to school together in Singapore? But Aunt Karly wanted to go to Holland and what would I do without Aunt Karly? And if my father wasn't going to be there, if he wasn't going to come, then I'd be better off accompanying her when she left for Holland. If she would let me. Of course, she would! Together, we were a family. And where else would I go?

Angrily, I kicked at another stone. Someone called my name. Did I hear that correctly? Yes, a man's voice was calling my name. I stopped in my tracks. There was only one person who called me that: 'Cornelia!'

No, I must be mistaken. It couldn't be him. Impossible! Just keep on walking. Stop imagining things. Again, I heard my name. A shiver ran down my spine from the top of my head to the tips of my toes. It was as if I were being electrified, and I couldn't go on. Slowly, I turned around. There, twenty metres away, stood my father. My father! I couldn't believe it was him. That he was really here. I put my hands over my eyes and took a deep breath. Only then did I dare to look again. Yes, the man was still there, and it was definitely him. That skinny man in his khaki shorts, sandals and a khaki shirt with rolled-up sleeves. That man, standing there on the desolate ground of Camp Wilhelmina, that man was my father.

I didn't go straight to him but looked at him from a distance. He looked well-groomed. His hair had gone grey, but it had been well-cut, and he had shaved. I walked towards him, nervously. For years, I had looked forward to this meeting, and now the time had come, I didn't know what to think. I felt numb.

'Cornelia!' called my father, 'How is my Nelly doing?' Just like he always used to, he put his arms around me, but I couldn't bear it. I didn't answer him, the way I used to but instead, I furiously escaped from his embrace and pummelled his chest with my two fists. 'Where were you?' I shouted with a catch in my throat. 'Why did it take you so long? Do you know how long I've been waiting for you? Three years and another three months since the camp. Why didn't you come before?'

My father didn't say anything and just held my arms with both hands. Slowly, the rage subsided. Now, I was just glad to see him again.

'What a lot of questions.' My father smiled and took my hand. He stroked it softly. 'I couldn't get here any sooner. I was taken to Japan as a prisoner of war and that's where I spent the war. After the capitulation, I was taken from Nagasaki to a camp in Manila in the Philippines and after that, I flew directly to Jakarta to find you.'

'It took you long enough to find us.'

'Much too long, you're right.'

'Yes.' I sighed and clamped my lips together. *Don't say anything*. I didn't want to say it. Not right now. But it was no use. My mouth whispered the words I didn't want to speak: 'Mummy is dead.'

My father pulled me to him and held me tight. We just stood there, in the open compound. Now I could bear being close to him. My head felt light and strange, as if I was flying through the clouds. I also felt the tension in his body. I noticed how he was almost falling apart himself and was struggling to stay upright. Then my father let me go and took a step back.

'I know about your mother. I read it in your letter.'

I shook my head. 'I didn't write about it to you.'

With his hand, my father wiped away the tears. 'No, but I understood when you, and not your mother, wrote back to me.'

'I couldn't tell you in that letter.'

'No, that would have been too much to ask.'

'My poor father,' I whispered, hoarsely.

'My poor Cornelia… and my poor Elenore,' sighed my father.

'And our poor family, too.'

My father held me tightly again and looked at me. 'I recognized you immediately.'

'Yes, well, here I am.'

'Yes, and at last, here am I, too.'

With my hand, I touched the material of his army shirt. 'You feel soft and smell new.'

'If only that were possible; to be new and start over!' sighed my father. He took a deep breath and carried on talking. 'You can smell my new clothes. In Manila, I bought stuff for myself and for you, too. It's military clothing, I couldn't get anything else. At the time, I didn't know Elenore wouldn't be needing them anymore.'

'It doesn't matter. I'm almost the same size as her now.'

'That's true. You've grown up. You're tall, too. I can hardly believe it.'

Akwardly, we walked on together across the compound.

'House number 344 is that way,' said my father and he pointed down a road to the left.

'How do you know I live there? You've only just got here.'

My father didn't say anything and just grinned his boy scout grin, that I knew so well from before. Together, we walked on. How long ago was it, since I had walked like this with my father? More than a million light years ago! I remembered San Francisco. How old was I then? Ten? My mother had taken a nap in the hotel and I had strolled with my father along a sunny boulevard with big palm trees. We had stopped to eat scoops of ice-cream from a crystal bowl in an Italian ice-cream parlour where everything shone and sparkled. That was another life. Or was it a dreamlife? Now, I was almost sixteen years old, and I was walking to my refugee shelter with my father. I was no longer a child, but a young woman. It felt odd, referring to myself as a young woman. In any case, I wasn't a little girl anymore.

Auntie had seen us coming from afar. I saw her waving at us madly with both arms over her head and as soon as my father reached the house, she flung herself around his neck.

'Peter Arends. My little brother! I knew you would come back. I knew it! I knew it! It was just a matter of time. How often did I say that? Ask Nelly!' I looked at Aunt Karly and my father. Brother and sister. They had the same straight posture and the same fluid way of moving their long arms and legs. My father wrapped his arms around his sister, picked her up and swung her around in a circle.

'Hey, Sis. Good to see you.' He was crying. I realized I had never seen him do that before.

'I'm sorry about Elenore, I'm so sorry I couldn't take better care of her,' sobbed my aunt, when my father had set her down on the ground again.

'Let the Japs be sorry about that,' said my father, grimly. He leant against the door of our refugee shelter. 'It's not your fault and you musn't blame yourself.'

It was hard to see my father and aunt being so emotional. In a minute, I would start crying, too, and I didn't want that. I dropped onto the bench in front of the house, next to Auntie.

'How did you finally find us?'

'The Red Cross traced me to the air-force, where I'm serving once again,' answered my father. 'I went to look for you in the harbour in Jakarta, where the ships arrive with evacuees from Surabaya. And then I found out that you had ended up here in Singapore.'

'The two of us together,' said Aunt Karly and she put an arm around me.

'Thank goodness! Auntie looked after mother when she was ill and then….' Once again, my voice refused to say that my mother was dead and I quickly went on: 'and then a week after the capitulation, Auntie and I walked out of the camp and travelled to Surabaya by train.'

'When it became too dangerous to stay in Surabaya, we were evacuated,' said Aunt Karly. 'We left for Singapore by ship. And you, Pete? Tell us. How did you get here?'

'By plane. Everything has changed because of the war, but I can still fly. I managed to arrange a flight as a co-pilot in a B-25 to Singapore. Tomorrow, we fly to Jakarta.'

'Jakarta?' asked Aunt Karly, going pale. 'Pete, you can't be serious? It's not safe there. Why don't you stay here?'

'It's my job. I'm the co-pilot on a B-25 and tomorrow, I'm flying back. And I'm taking Nell with me. After that, I'll be back as soon as I can to fetch you, Sis.'

I moved along the bench, closer to Aunt Karly. The thought of having to leave her behind here was unbearable. 'I'm not going back to Jakarta without Aunt Karly,' I protested. 'Ever since we ended up in Camp Ambarawa, we've been together every hour of the day. That's been more than three years.'

'There's no other way. I can only take along one person, and that's you.'

Furiously, I looked at my father. 'Then you might as well not have found me, because if Auntie can't go, I'm not going either! I want to stay with you, Auntie!' I looked at my aunt, pleadingly. She tried to reassure me. 'Nell, don't you remember how much you longed to see your father and how, every day, we went to enquire if there was any news of him? Well, he's here now, and I think it's a good idea that you go with him. You can get used to being together again. We'll see each other again soon, I'm sure of that. Your father will fetch me as soon as he can. That's what you said, right, Pete?'

My father nodded. 'Absolutely!'

'I think it's really stupid, you defending him!' I shouted angrily. 'I don't have a choice. If my father wants me to go with him, I have to do as I'm told, but you could explain to him that it's better if I stay here with you.'

'I can't do that, Nelly. He's your father. And you can't tell your father, who has just found you, that you'd rather not go with him.'

'I would like to take you with me, Cornelia,' said my father.

I sighed. I had imagined the reunion with my father so differently. I wasn't happy at all and I felt like I was going to explode at any minute.

'We've got an afternoon and an evening together to say goodbye,' said Aunt Karly and she tried to look me in the face.

I looked away. 'I'm going to see someone for a moment.'

'Boyfriend?' asked my father.

'Of course not! I don't have a boyfriend.'

'So, there are no boys here that you like? That's hard to believe.'

I jumped up from the bench. There was no way I was going to tell my father about Tim. As unobtrusively as possible, I touched the ring that hung by its cord around my neck. I didn't even know if I would ever see Tim again. It was none of my father's business. Especially if he wasn't going to take any notice of what I wanted. I just couldn't stand up to my father and I didn't want to start a fight. 'I'm going to talk to Lisa. I know her from the Ambarawa Camp.'

'Do you have to go right now?' asked Auntie. 'Do you really want to leave now when your father has only just got here? Stay here with us.'

'I have to say goodbye before I'm sent to Jakarta, don't I! When we left Ambarawa, I wasn't able to say goodbye, either.'

'You won't be too long?' she asked, in a concerned voice.

I didn't answer and walked away. I could feel my father and Aunt Karly watching me go. No-one forbade me to go. I didn't want to walk away, but I did, anyway.

November 12th was a stupid day. It wasn't just the day Leon Trotsky was expelled from the Russian Communist Party, but it was also the day my father took me away and put an end to the life I shared with Aunt Karly. I couldn't understand why Aunt Karly consented. Well anyway, she didn't do anything to prevent it.

DON'T MAKE ME DO THINGS

'Where's the airfield?' I asked my father as we were getting ready to leave. It was six o'clock in the morning and it was another hour until dawn. Since yesterday, I had hardly spoken with my father or Aunt Karly. When I got back from my visit to Lisa, it had been almost dark. We had sat outside on the veranda for a bit. There was no mention of our imminent departure. I didn't know how to broach the subject. I was sorry about that, now. I didn't like being made to do things, but I should have stayed and not run off to Lisa. I should have talked to them. I should have convinced my father not to take me to Jakarta, but to leave me here with Karly until we could go with him together. Now I wished I had gone about things differently. And now that everything had run its course, and we were at the point of departure, I couldn't think of anything more meaningful to ask than something about the position of the airfield.

'One degree twenty-five minutes North, and one hundred and three degrees and fifty-two minutes East,' my father answered stoically. He clearly didn't feel like having a conversation. He didn't want to be conciliatory. He, too, was finding it difficult to say goodbye to Aunt Karly.

'The Seletar Airfield is to the North-East of Singapore,' explained Auntie. 'It's not a long drive.' She smiled and wrapped her arms around me. I stiffened, but when I turned around and saw her smiling, I relaxed.

'Must I really go without you?' I asked, already knowing the answer. If I had come home earlier yesterday, I might have talked her out of it. Now it was too late. *Stupid*. I felt tears pricking behind my eyes and tried to think of something else. I didn't want to cry.

'Yes, sweetheart, you must. And even if you're thinking that you should have convinced me yesterday, you must know, that you wouldn't have succeeded. We're going to see each other again soon, and meanwhile, we're going to write to each other often.' For a moment, Aunt Karly held me very, very tightly and kissed me on the forehead before letting me go. There was no-one who knew me as well as she did.

'I'm not patient enough to wait for the post. You know that.'

'That's true, but the war is over. I'm sure letters will be delivered faster now.'

'What if Tim turns up here?' I whispered.

'Then I'll make sure he finds you!' Auntie hugged me one more time, and then things happened quickly. Before I knew it, my *bungkusan* with my things was in the back of the jeep, I was sitting next to my father and we were driving out of Camp Wilhelmina. The sun was rising and the sky coloured red in the first morning light. It was such a beautiful morning, despite it feeling as if this was the worst day of my life. It had to be a bad sign, that red morning light, I was convinced of that. I'd never see Aunt Karly again. That was a terrible thing! At the same time, I had to go with my father. Perhaps a part of me wanted to go with my father? Away from here. Was that a bad thing?

'Beautiful morning,' said my father. 'That's a good sign!'

My father and I lived on different planets.

It was only a short drive to Seletar airfield. It wasn't much, that airfield. In my eyes, it was not much more than a large, bare field.

'Do you see those old crates over there?' asked my father.

I knew what he wanted me to tell him. 'Mmm... Mosquitos and small Dakotas and of course, the B-25 that you came in.'

'Well done! I knew that you wouldn't disappoint me.' He nodded approvingly and immediately seemed to be in a better mood. The pilot was ready and waiting in the cockpit. My father took his seat as co-pilot and, as an exception, I was allowed to sit somewhere at the back of the cockpit.

'A beautiful morning for flying,' said my father, 'you don't often get such a clear view over the sea.'

The engines of the B-25 throbbed into life and then we took off.

JAKARTA IS NOT FOR GIRLS

Jakarta was a disappointment. Very occasionally, my father took me into town. The streets were dirty and rundown. Lots of things were broken. The canals were dirty. My father had rented two rooms in the Netherlands Hotel. A room for him, and one for me. He worked all the time. Early in the morning, he would poke his head round my door and call: 'I'm off to work. Have a nice day, Nell,' and then he was gone. I didn't see him all day. I had breakfast on my own and in the evening, we had dinner together in the restaurant of the hotel. My father was really kind to me, and he was trying very hard, but I also felt his impatience. He wasn't used to spending so much time with me.

'May I go into town when you're at work?' I asked after two days.

'Who would you go with?'

'By myself. I don't know anyone here.'

'You can't go out on your own. It's not safe here.'

'Then what am I supposed to do all day?'

'You're not going out on your own. Stay in the hotel or in the garden and read a book. That won't hurt you.' As far as my father was concerned, the matter was closed. But I was bored. I missed Lisa, and – something I would never have thought – I even missed Camp Wilhelmina! At least there I could wander around freely.

I often thought of Aunt Karly. I missed her so much that I now started dreaming about her as well as my mother. The post-war aunt that is. I dreamt we were on the train together, in the same kind of third-class carriage in which we had travelled to Surabaya, and that Aunt Karly called out, 'This train will soon be arriving in Amsterdam!' That made us laugh out loud because that was impossible, of course. We'd never been to Amsterdam, although we'd really like to go. That's what Aunt Karly really wanted, in any case, and so did I. I tried not to wake up from the dream, but of course that happened anyway, and then I was alone in my room feeling lonelier than I'd ever felt before. What would my mother have thought? *Shush, don't think of that.*

I found a worn copy of *Max Havelaar* by Eduard Douwes Dekker. That book told the story of the fifteen-year-old Javanese, Saïdjah, and his sweetheart, Adinda. When I was a child, I used to ask my father to read me that story again and again. I never tired of hearing how Saïdjah was forced to go looking for work in Jakarta, far away from his sweetheart. Homesick, he wrote a poem that I still knew off-by-heart. In the camp, if I couldn't sleep, I used to think of this poem, and then it used to feel as if my father was a little bit closer to me.

If I die in Badur

And I am buried outside the village

Eastwards against the hill

Where the grass is tall,

Then Adinda shall pass through there

And the edge of her sarong will

Softly move along the grass....

I shall hear that.

Now these words of longing didn't make me think of my father, but of Tim. The tale of Saïdjah and Adinda didn't end well. When he came back, thirty-six moons later, Saïdjah found the bodies of his lover Adinda, and her father. They had been killed by the Dutch army. Saïdjah then committed suicide. In his book, Douwes Dekker stood up for the Indonesians. What would he say if he saw the Indies now?

If I wasn't reading, I talked to the guests in the hotel.

'Are you alright? Aren't you bored, on your own?' people always asked.

'I'm fine,' I usually answered. 'I'm not alone, because I'm here with my father.' I tried not to bother anyone. I wandered around a bit in the enclosed garden of the hotel and told myself that things would change. That my father would have more time once he had done what he had to do. Or that Tim would find me here and would take me to a beautiful spot in the mountains, where it was safe and where, at last, I would be able to kiss him. That thought made me happy for a moment, but, of course, it was never going to happen. Most of all, I just felt very lonely.

My father wasn't happy with the situation, either.

'You can't stay here,' he admitted after two weeks, on one of the few occasions when we walked through Jakarta together. 'I was wrong. Jakarta is not for girls, and I'm working.'

'But I want to stay with you in the Netherlands Hotel, I objected. 'I'm doing fine. I just got here, and I don't want to go.'

'I know that, but this is no place for young girls. It's not safe. Much less safe than I thought it would be.'

'But you wanted me to go with you to Jakarta. You brought me here.' I stopped in the middle of the street and tried not to get angry, but I could feel my insides trembling.

'I wanted to have you close, after all that time that I had to do without you. Is that so strange?'

'No, but now I'm with you, you don't have any time for me. You found me, and now you want to send me away again. I think that's really unfair.'

'It's harder than I thought. I don't have enough time. I think it would be better if you went to Australia,' said my father. 'I'll follow you there as soon as I can.'

'And Aunt Karly? You were going to pick her up from the Wilhelmina Camp, weren't you? Does she have to stay there now?' It was busy in the street and my father pulled me over to the shadowy part of the square.

'I asked her whether she wanted to come to Australia, but she has put her name down on a list for repatriation to Holland. I can't understand what she's going to do there,' said my father, disgruntled. 'She's never been there.'

I didn't want to tell him that Aunt Karly wanted to meet the Dutch family of her fiancé. Certainly not now I was so angry. I thought of Tim. If my father sent me to Australia, there was absolutely no chance that I would ever see him again.

'You should have left me with Aunt Karly if you're going to send me to Australia now. Auntie would never have left Camp Wilhelmina without me. If she goes to Holland, I'll probably never see her again.' I walked on, angrily.

My father followed me. 'I would like to keep you here, Cornelia.' He looked so tired and there were sharp lines etched into his face. It made him look old. 'I would like to keep you here, but it's not good for you here. All the young people from here are going to Australia. It's safer there. You'll like it there.'

'And will you be coming to Australia? You don't spend any time with me now. Why would you in Australia?' We were back at the hotel.

'Of course, I'm going to join you there. I'll finish a few things here first and then I'll go on leave for a few months.' My father held the door to the entrance open for me. 'Really! I promise! We'll celebrate Christmas together.'

I still didn't say anything and walked into the hotel. I was angry, but I also knew that it was no use arguing. I wasn't yet eighteen and I had to do what my father said.

It took a while to arrange my departure from Jakarta. I wrote lots of letters to Aunt Karly and Lisa. I received an answer from Auntie. She said she missed me, too, and wished things were different. She also wrote that it wasn't easy for my father. Aunt Karly was waiting for a berth on a ship to Holland. I didn't want her to go. I already really missed her, and if she were to board that ship, she would be travelling ever further away from me. Lisa wrote to me that she was going to make enquiries about Tim in Singapore. Perhaps he would surface there. I felt empty and slept a lot.

'I've got everything organized,' my father announced cheerfully at the end of November, as we were having dinner together in the Netherlands Hotel. He had always been really good at pretending there was nothing the matter.

'On 1st December, you'll fly to Australia with Captain Somers in a B-25, with a stop-over in Biak. A week later, I'll be coming to Australia, too. Somers is a friend and a colleague of mine and he'll take good care of you. Pretty neat, don't you think?'

'Does it matter what I think?' I was surprised at how calmly I managed to ask that question, even though my heart was racing.

'You'll be happy there,' said my father.

My stomach cramped. I wanted to scream and smash the plates on the table, but I knew there was no point in objecting. 'Why can't we travel to Australia together?'

'I can't leave any earlier and I don't want you to stay in Jakarta any longer.'

'That's what you say. It's a matter of choices.'

'Good,' concluded my father, 'so we're agreed.' He was satisfied. He preferred to decide things for himself. Quite different to Aunt Karly, who was always open to my ideas or wishes. My father was more of a dictator. I could only do as he bade. Otherwise he would be furious at me. For now, I resigned myself to it.

On the day of my departure, my father went to work. In the morning, he came to say goodbye. I was still in bed and pretended to be asleep. He left without saying anything.

The flight from Jakarta to the island of Biak went smoothly. Captain Somers was an easy-going man of around forty. 'Travelling all alone, that can't be easy, my girl,' he said as I boarded the plane.

'I'm used to it.' I could sense that he felt sorry for me and that only made me act more bravely than I was feeling. It was still light when we started our descent, and shortly after we had landed at the small airfield of Biak. Captain Somers showed me to the room where I would spend the night, and then he took me along to the officers' mess in the big bamboo hut on the beach. It was almost empty inside. There was just a group of young officers standing by the door.

Impatiently, Somers ordered two lemonades and when our order came, he quickly took one sip, put his glass down and pushed back his cane chair. 'I need to make some arrangements. I'll see you tomorrow,' he said, and he was gone before I could say goodbye. I emptied my glass in two gulps. I was still thirsty. Was there anyone watching? No, I didn't think so. I took Somers's glass and drank down the now lukewarm lemonade. I looked at the officers, still standing by the door – and then I saw Tim. He was standing with his back to me and was shuffling his feet impatiently. His long dark hair had been cut short and wasn't sticking up in all directions anymore. My heart was beating faster, and I felt light in my head. In a daze, I walked across the room towards him and tapped him gently on the shoulder. 'Tim!'

He turned around, and I was looking into the friendly blue eyes of an English officer. 'Can I help you, Miss?'

I wished the ground could have swallowed me up. 'Sorry,' I whispered, and ran out of the officers' mess. I went as far as I could, away from everyone, down onto the beach. *Stupid! Stupid! Stupid!* How could I have been so mistaken? It was out of the question that Tim could even be here! At the water's edge, I dropped onto the beach and stretched out in the warm sand.

'Hi, can I sit next to you?' The young officer whom I had tapped on the shoulder, had followed me, and flopped down next to me. I shot up.

'I'm sorry I'm not who you thought I was,' he said, smiling. 'I'm Jamie Twist, co-pilot.'

I smiled back, shyly. I felt myself blush, but luckily you couldn't see that in the dusk. 'I'm Nell Arends. Yes, sorry, so silly of me. I really thought you were Tim – you look like him and you're probably the same age.'

'I'm eighteen, and how old is that brother of yours?'

'Seventeen.' I should have said that it wasn't my brother, but for some reason, I didn't. 'I've just arrived from Jakarta with Captain Somers. He's a colleague of my father's.'

'Yes, I know him, but I don't know your father. Where are you going?'

'Tomorrow, I fly to Australia with Somers, to Sydney, and then I'm going on to Bondi, a beach resort not far from there.'

'Yes, I know Bondi. So, you like the sea? Of course, you like the sea. All pretty girls like the sea.'

I pretended I hadn't heard that last bit. 'I've no idea. I've never been to Bondi. My father has promised to follow me there soon.'

'It sounds like you're not sure whether he'll come. What will you do if he doesn't show up?'

I laughed nervously. What kind of a question was that? Was Jamie joking?

'I'm sure my father will show up. But if he does come to Bondi, I don't know what good that will do me.' I sighed. I didn't want to say this at all, but I just couldn't keep my mouth shut. The words went their own way. 'My life is a mess. My mother is dead, I haven't seen my father for more than three years, but he still doesn't have time for me. My favourite aunt is on her way to Holland, the boy you look like has disappeared on Java, and I don't know where I belong anymore.'

Jamie picked up a shell from the sand, turned it around in his hands and then threw it away. 'It's the war, it does a lot of damage and confuses people. I'm sure you'll like it in Bondi. The sea there is just like here. The sea can heal people. On a beautiful evening like this, you should go for a swim.'

'Maybe.'

'I'm going in, anyway.' Before I knew it, he had jumped up and tossed his clothes in a heap. I watched him run across the white sand into the sea and disappear beneath the waves. Naked!

Speechless, I walked to the edge of the water until it covered my ankles. The waves washed softly over my feet. Unexpectedly, the water was lovely and warm. I looked around me. Did I dare? I walked back to the beach and laid my clothes on the sand. Then I took a deep breath and ran into the sea, dived deep and let myself be carried by the water. This had to be paradise on earth. I had never swum at night before. Let alone naked!

A second later, Jamie appeared right in front of me in the water. He looked at me, smiling. His head was very close to mine. Our foreheads were almost touching. I could see drops of water hanging from his long lashes. His mouth looked like Tim's, although it didn't curl up at the corners. I could feel my heart thudding like mad. I didn't dare look at Jamie anymore and closed my eyes. For a split second, his lips touched mine and then he disappeared under the water. A little more to the side, he popped up again. 'You will love Bondi. You are like a mermaid; so beautiful,' he said, and with big strokes he swam in the direction of the beach.

I stayed in the sea and watched him, spellbound. I ran my tongue over my lips. I tasted salt and nothing else special. Was this a kiss? Had I now kissed someone? Or had I imagined it? Perhaps it wasn't a kiss, his lips had never touched mine, he had just said I was as beautiful as a mermaid and I had made up the rest? And if I had kissed a boy, what did that say about me? I wanted Tim to kiss me, didn't I?

Back in bed, the moment my wet head touched the pillow, I fell asleep. I dreamt I was sitting naked on the beach. My mother was combing my hair and plaiting it with scented orchids. She felt very alive and very close. 'He really loves you, that boy,' said my mother. 'He's a fine young man. Treasure that. You don't often meet a good one in life,' and then my mother walked into the sea.

'Stay with me!' I cried. I wanted to ask her who she meant: Tim or Jamie, but she didn't listen. She waved at me, and suddenly, she was gone. The orchids in my hair immediately wilted. I woke up crying. My hair smelt of the sea.

BONDI: THE PLACE TO BE

'You've come!' I said, when my father appeared at the door on 14th December. I could hardly believe he was here.

'You knew I would. That's what we agreed. I rented rooms for both of us here in Bondi. You were to travel ahead, and I was to come a week later, that's what I promised you when you left.'

'Yes, but I wasn't sure you would really come.'

'If I make a promise, Cornelia, then I will keep it,' my father replied, offended by my lack of faith in him.

I didn't mention that he'd come not one, but two weeks later, and smiled vaguely. I thought of my lonely weeks in the Netherlands Hotel in Jakarta. Looking back from merry Bondi, I found that period increasingly depressing. Hadn't my father also promised we would have a good time together in Jakarta? Or had I just imagined that?

'You're daydreaming,' said my father, and went inside. 'I've taken three months' leave to be here with you. That's something I'm really looking forward to. You look well, Cornelia. You've got some colour from being outside and your hair is shiny and more curly.'

'I'm at the beach a lot.'

'That's just around the corner, of course. And the house? Do you like the house?'

I nodded. 'It's beautiful.' And it really was. The house where we lived belonged to Mrs Bond. I didn't make that name up: Mrs Bond from Bondi. That was really her name. For the sake of ease, I just called her Bondy. The house was at Warners Avenue in Bondi at a few minutes' walk from the beach. Straight on down the street and you reached the water. From the house, you could hear the surf breaking. All day long, there was a lovely breeze and the temperature was very pleasant. It was a modern house with lots of rooms full of light. I lived with my father on the top floor.

'It's beautiful,' I repeated, as I went ahead of my father up the stairs. 'We have two rooms, a bathroom and a toilet. Bondy does the cooking for us. She's not at home at the moment.' I threw open the door to his room and my father set his suitcase down on the big mahogany bed. It had a monumental headpiece that was decorated with large flowers cut from wood. Then I went into my room. 'This is where I sleep, in the room with the bay window. I would love to sleep in that extension. If you sit there, you can see the sea.'

'The nicest spots are always claimed first. It was like that in the camp, too,' said my father.

We looked at each other a little awkwardly. I knew he had meant it as a joke, but it wasn't funny. It was the first time my father had said anything about what he had been through. We had never talked about his captivity in Japan, or about my mother's, Aunt Karly's, or my time in the camp.

'It's alright if you want to swap,' I offered as a gesture.

'Don't be silly. It's fine like this. And you're right. It's a beautiful room with that view. Not only can you hear the sea, but you can see it too. I think I can even smell the sea.'

'You can sit in the bay window if you like. As often as you want,' I offered, and showed him the bathroom. For a long time, we admired the bathroom and the clean toilet with running water.

'What a delightful luxury: a toilet so clean you could safely drink from it.' My father flushed the toilet and cried enthusiastically: 'Look how clean the water is, and we have it all to ourselves!'

For a moment, I was afraid he was really going to drink the water from the toilet to prove his point. That wasn't his intention, of course, but I wasn't used to my father's odd sense of humour. I left the bathroom. 'And every week, there are clean sheets. Now that's what I call luxury! And we have lovely meals every day, because Bondy likes cooking.'

'Good, then Wendy was right.'

'Wendy? Do I know her?'

'That's someone from the airbase. She recommended this place.'

'I didn't know that. Well, Bondi is the place to be! I never expected life would be so good again, or that I'd be so happy in a place that I definitely didn't want to go to. I'm happier than I have been in a long time. You can just go for a walk here. I can go anywhere without having to be afraid.'

'Show me this paradise of yours, then,' said my father, smiling.

'Hi Neal, how are you today?' Nathan looked at me with his dazzling smile. He was irresistible when he smiled like that. It wasn't just his mouth that smiled, but also his eyes and the tip of his nose; his whole face shone with joy.

The way he pronounced my name made me laugh. It was as if I was more aware of that than usual, now that I was standing here with my father.

I had walked down Warners Avenue with my father to the beach at the North Bondi Surf Life Saving Club. It only took a minute. I had told my father that, before he came, I had gone to the beach here every day. I hadn't told him that I came here mostly to meet the people at the club, with whom I'd quickly made friends. Lots of young people came here and they were all really nice and open towards newcomers. The boys and girls also all flirted with each other! It's true. Not always in a serious way, more for a laugh. I had never experienced that before, and it made me feel very self-conscious. But it was also great fun, although I didn't really dare flirt back. I knew a few people at the club a little better, now. One of them was Nathan, whom we had just met. Blond, cropped hair, bright blue eyes, athletic body from all the swimming: the biggest flirt of them all. We often swam together. Swimming wasn't the same as flirting. But now that I was thinking it over, standing next to my father, I wasn't so sure anymore if that was true. After all, I knew nothing about flirting. Certainly not compared to the boys and girls of the North Bondi Surf Life Saving Club, who seemed to have been doing that forever. Perhaps going for a swim together was a bit like flirting, after all?

'Everything alright?' Again, Nathan looked at me, grinning.

'Yes, fine... Thanks Nathan, for asking. This is my father. He's just arrived here from Jakarta.'

My father shook Nathan's hand jovially. They were the same height. The boy and the man. I knew Nathan was just as old as I was, almost sixteen. And my father, how old would my father be? Stupid that I didn't know that anymore. Thirty-seven? Thirty-eight? What would Nathan look like in twenty years' time?

'Lovely spot you have here,' said my father. 'Important work, pulling people out of the water. Are you a member of the life-saving brigade, too?'

'Almost,' answered Nathan, enthusiastically. 'I'm practicing for the bronze medal. Once I have bronze, I can go into the sea. At the moment, I'm scheduled for the beach patrol to make sure people swim in the safe zone, between the flags. That's how I know Neal, from when I had to fish her out of the sea.'

I went bright red. Bigmouth. Why did that show-off have to go and tell my father that? Now I might not be allowed to go to the beach anymore. Just imagine. 'I didn't know then that there are some parts of the beach where you weren't supposed to swim,' I defended myself. 'I really won't do it again.' My father wasn't listening. All his attention was focussed on Nathan.

'Nell was lucky that you were on the beach.'

'Next time, I'll rescue your daughter with the Surfboat,' boasted Nathan. 'Right, Neal?'

I didn't say anything, and just felt myself getting redder and redder. I wanted to move on, but my father wouldn't let up. 'Do you also have boats, then?'

'Yes, a couple. Just recently, we got a new one, the *Astral*. I can go on that once I have bronze. Neal should train for bronze, too. With her long legs, she has a real talent for swimming. They're beautiful legs, too.' He said that last bit with a grin on his face, and so softly that only I could hear.

'Is that so? Are you really such a good swimmer?' My father looked questioningly at me.

'You know that I am! When I was young, I was awarded every swimming certificate that was going.'

'That's true,' said my father, but I could tell by his voice that he couldn't remember. Had I made it up, then, that my father and mother used to come to the swimming pool when we swam for certificates?

'I'm going to work out, will you swim along?' asked Nathan.

I shrugged. Today, I suddenly found him really annoying, but I still smiled at him. 'I can't today. My father just got here.'

'Too bad,' said Nathan, and shook my father's hand. 'Nice to meet you, Sir.' He took off his cap and waved goodbye with it. Then he put it back on his head and was gone.

I walked further along the beach with my father.

'You've really turned that boy's head.'

'Don't be silly. I hardly know him.'

'You don't need to, but that Nathan really likes you, take it from me.'

In silence, we walked on. My father was in a merry mood.

'When I lived in England for a year, I played tennis every day with John, the son of the family where I was staying. John and his girlfriend Eva played against me and Elenore – Eva's friend. That's how I met your mother. After the first match, I fell madly in love with her, and she hadn't an inkling.'

I didn't know what to say to my father. I knew the story. Not from my father, but my mother had often told me how she had met my father. Love at first sight is what she called it. I put my arm through my father's, and we walked on like this, each thinking our own thoughts. For a moment, we were very close to each other, and to my mother. But after a little while, my father pulled his arm back. 'Do you have a swimming costume?' he asked. 'I suppose you must have since you're doing so much swimming.'

I nodded. 'Bondy gave me one.'

'Bondy? Do I know her?'

'Mrs Bond, I told you, I call her Bondy.'

'Oh yes, so you did,' said my father, 'I forgot'.

'She gave me one. It used to belong to her daughter.' I didn't tell my father it was a bikini, just like all the other girls wore here.

In the distance, I could see Nathan running into the water. *So, Nathan was in love, was he? How could my father tell?*

No. Failed again. She had disappeared. When I opened my eyes, I was on my own again in the big bed in the bay window. The day my father arrived, after our visit to the beach, we had moved my bed there together. My father thought it silly, but I had bugged him constantly, and when I promised that he could just sit around for the rest of the day and didn't have to go out with me again, he finally relented and helped me move the bed.

'I told you so,' said my father, when, after a lot of effort, we had moved the bed. 'Now there's no room to stand, and you'll have to climb in over the foot of the bed.'

'It doesn't matter,' I cried. 'I think it's a fantastic place to sleep.' My father had to admit that that was true after he'd lain next to me for a minute on my bed in the bay window.

Now that I could sleep in the bay window, the nights were fantastic. The small enclosed space made me feel very safe. In the evening, the sound of the sea rocked me to sleep. The waves carried me far away to the unknown, where everything was quiet and peaceful, and where my mother was very close by. Sometimes, she came and lay down beside me. She didn't say anything but just held my hand and we breathed in and out together in the same rhythm. In and out. I tried to lie as still as possible, because I was afraid that an unexpected movement would startle her and make her disappear, and I wanted her to stay until morning. I wanted to be washed up on the beach with her, to let the sun warm our bodies and then, when we had woken up to the dawning of a new day, to talk to her. But I didn't lie still enough, and every morning, I woke up alone, in bed.

This morning, too, just for a moment, my mother felt very close, but as soon as I opened my eyes, that feeling was gone. The door to my room was half open. I heard my father talking to Bondy. Or rather, it was Bondy who was doing the talking. 'She is a lovely girl, always smiling and very pretty.'

I knew she couldn't see me and didn't know I could hear her, but still I blushed bright red from those words of praise. I didn't dare get up to close the door. She would know immediately that I had overheard her.

First, my father mumbled something. I couldn't really hear it, and then he said: 'She has her mother's looks. Especially now that she's older, and almost the same age as my wife when I first met her. And sometimes, the resemblance is too much to bear...'

'I can imagine that. That can't always be easy for you,' said Bondy.

The voices died away and I heard my father and Bondy going down the stairs. Frozen, I lay in bed. I already knew I looked like my mother, Aunt Karly had told me that, too. She'd liked that. 'In a few years' time, you'll look just like Elenore when she had you. If you miss her, you only have to look in the mirror and you'll know what she looked like when you were little. And later, when you're sixty, I'll know what Elenore would have looked like if she had reached that age.'

It was only now that I realized that that resemblance was difficult for my father.

This past week, I had spent lots of time with my father. That was lovely, but also complicated. One moment we got on fine and talked like friends. The next moment, for no apparent reason, he was moody and short-tempered, and he would suddenly act all authoritarian. And I couldn't remember having heard him laugh. We weren't used to spending so much time together, and sometimes my father thought I was still his little girl from before the war. That's when we clashed. Or perhaps he got upset whenever I reminded him of my mother? If only Aunt Karly was here, then I could ask her if she knew what was going on with my father but I hadn't had a letter from her for ten days now, and she usually wrote to me every other day.

I ought to go downstairs. I was going to Sydney with my father to see the Christmas decorations there. But now, that seemed like an impossible task. I didn't want my father to know that I had overheard him, but nor could I act as if I hadn't heard anything.

'Cornelia, we're leaving in one minute!' called my father impatiently.

I got up and left my safe bay window.

SURPRISE

'We're catching the train to Central Station,' said my father. 'Apparently, that's where the most beautiful Christmas lights of Sydney are.'

Now that I was outside, I was looking forward to the trip with my father and I set a smart pace. I walked so fast that I was always a metre or two ahead of him. We had only just left and were walking along Warners Avenue somewhere between Gould Street and Wairoa Avenue, when a Ford pulled up beside us and then parked a few metres ahead. The engine stopped and the driver got out. It was a young woman with thin bleached hair that she wore pinned up. She opened her arms wide and then walked towards my father with hips swaying. Her heels click-clacked on the street. She smiled at my father, shook his hand, and then gave him the car keys. 'Have fun,' she said, and disappeared in the direction from which we had just come.

My father glowed with pleasure and held the car keys aloft. 'May I offer you a drive in this car, Madam?' He held the car door open and ushered me in.

'Who was that?' I asked curiously, as we drove off.

'Wendy Wagner, someone I know from the airbase.'

'The one who advised you about our house in Bondi?'

'Yes. And she's letting me use this Ford. I thought it would be more fun than the tram,' explained my father, once we had picked up speed. 'Don't you think it's like my old Ford from before the war?'

I nodded although I couldn't recall that particular car. I hadn't sat in a normal car for ages. In trucks, yes, and in other army vehicles, but not in a Ford. I did remember the Ford we'd had to drive across America and I imagined driving across Australia with my father in this one.

'Are we still going to the Central Station in Sydney or are we just going to drive to the other side of Australia?'

My father laughed and accelerated again. 'I'm afraid we'll be sticking to Sydney for the time being.'

We didn't talk much in the car. The Ford seemed to drive by itself, so smoothly did my father let the wheel glide through his hands and manoeuvre the car along the roads. I closed my eyes and I was ten years old again and we were driving somewhere in Death Valley, America, while my mother slept in the back of the car. The war in Asia was still a long way off.

I didn't dare ask my father, but I was sure that he was thinking of our pre-war trip across America, too. It could hardly be otherwise. Now, everything was different. I was sitting beside my father as we drove down Oxford Street, Moore Park Road, Foveaux Street to Central Station and Eddy Avenue where my father parked the car. I could smell the trains. Life went on. My father and I had survived the war. My mother hadn't. My mother lay alone and deserted in a field in Ambarawa. I had to talk to my father about that because she couldn't be left there. I had to talk to him about how much I missed her.

I had to run after my father who was already striding towards the concourse. By the time I caught up with him, he had already reached the entrance. We went in together. It was a huge station. There weren't many Christmas decorations to be seen, just a few paper stars. I was about to say something about that to my father when I caught sight of her standing beneath the great clock that hung in the station. I couldn't believe it, but it was really her: Aunt Karly! My Aunt Karly!

Zigzagging through the crowds, I ran across the station towards her and leapt into her arms. I clung to her as if I was afraid this meeting was a dream, that Aunt Karly and the station would dissolve, and I would wake up in my bed in the bay window. But it wasn't a dream and the realization made me burst into tears. Aunt Karly couldn't hold back her tears either, and we stood holding each other and crying in the middle of that huge station in Sydney, while my father awkwardly stood nearby. That made me laugh out loud. I let go of Aunt Karly and wiped away my tears. 'Sorry... I'm a bit mixed up, I'm so glad I can hug you again.'

'Good to see you, Nelly', said Aunt Karly.

I laughed and hugged my aunt again. 'So, this is why we came here?'

My father put his hands up in the air. 'Of course, I knew that Karly was coming to Sydney.'

'And you didn't say anything?' I cried, in disbelief.

'I wanted to surprise you, Nell,' said my father. He gestured apologetically with his hands. I wanted to say something back, but Aunt Karly took both my hands in hers and said, 'And it is a surprise, isn't it, Nell!' I sensed the emphasis with which she chose her words. It made me smile and I could feel the tightness inside me softening. She was right. I didn't have to get angry. My father had meant well. There was nothing wrong with surprises. I gave my father a kiss on his cheek. 'It certainly is. I was taken completely by surprise. Thank you very much.'

'Let's go,' said Aunt Karly. 'After all you've written me, Nell, I really want to see where you live.'

Whereas the trip into Sydney had been coloured with homesickness and longing for my mother, the journey back was merry and full of energy. In the car, Aunt Karly sat in the front with my father. Sitting in the back, I leant forward between the two front seats. Auntie sat half-turned towards me so that it was just as if I were sitting in the front of the car in between Auntie and my father. Aunt Karly and I chatted away. 'How did you get here, how did you do it?' I asked.

'A freighter from Singapore brought me here and then someone dropped me off at the station. Your father organized that last part. Now I can spend Christmas and the New Year with you. On 2nd January…'

'No, don't tell me, don't tell me…' I cried. 'I don't want to hear that you're leaving again on 2nd January.'

'Now you've said it yourself,' she laughed. 'And yes, I'll be taking the boat to the Netherlands.'

'Stay! Please stay. Bondi is the place to be! No, don't say anything. I know you're going to Holland. And so you should. Of course, you should, and I do understand. Let's celebrate and talk until you board the ship. I'm going to savour every minute you're here. I've missed you so terribly.'

'And I you, but you can manage without me because you look wonderfully well, Nelly.'

I drummed my hands on her shoulders. 'I can't manage without you at all! You know that!'

'You know I'm joking! But I'm so pleased to see you like this. You've got a lovely tan. I can see you spend lots of time outdoors and you're not so skinny anymore.'

'I've got a bottom again and the beginning of breasts. Even had a period.'

'Nell! You shouldn't say such things,' grumbled my father. 'I don't want to hear all that. Those are the kind of things a daughter discusses with her mother.' He clenched his fist and furiously thumped the horn, in the middle of the steering wheel.

Aunt Karly put her hand on my father's arm. 'I'm sorry, Peter. Nell and I aren't used to talking in the company of men, friends, brothers, fathers, husbands anymore.'

'Are you saying that as a reproach?' asked my father, sullenly.

'Of course not. What makes you say that? It's just an observation. Camps for women. Camps for men. Because of that infernal war, we're not used to each other's company anymore. And because that war is rooted inside all of us, it will take a while before it all gets back to normal.'

Aunt Karly turned around and nodded reassuringly at me. 'You've become a beautiful woman, Nell!'

'Maybe so,' said my father and he hit the accelerator again. The car shot forward.

I wondered what my father meant by that. Was it about the woman I had become or the war that was in everyone? The conversation in the car faltered. The silence hung like a dark evening mist around us. I felt uncomfortable at how the conversation had developed. It was unpleasant to see that I reminded my father of my mother at the most unpredictable moments. Especially of my mother's absence. I couldn't stand the silence anymore and started talking to Aunt Karly about something else. 'How is Lisa? Have you heard anything about her? Do you know I even wished we were back in Camp Wilhelmina? Especially when I was in Jakarta. That was when I really wanted to be with you again, just for a little while.'

'Lisa is fine. She's going to Holland, too, to visit her family.'

'I'm glad for her, that she found her family.' I also wondered if Lisa had found out anything about Tim. She had been going to ask his family about him for me. But I'd ask Auntie about that some other time. 'Wow Auntie, it's like a dream that you're here and just sitting next to me!'

'I know, I know! I can't believe it myself. And it's thanks to your father. He made a lot of arrangements for me, so I could be here for Christmas.'

I saw Aunt Karly smiling at my father, who had been wanting to say something for a while now. This was his chance and he quickly chipped in: 'I missed you too, Sis! I'm glad you'll be staying at our inn for Christmas.' He wanted to say more, but when Aunt Karly and I started rattling on again to each other, he gave up. There was just so much to catch up on.

'You'll be sleeping in my room,' I said to Aunt Karly, when we went into our house at Warners Avenue. I carried her suitcase up the stairs and dragged it into my room.

'Not just in your room, but also in your bed,' observed Aunt Karly.

'You don't mind, do you?' I asked, anxiously.

'No darling, of course not. It'll be fun. A bit like the old days.'

I breathed a sigh of relief and sprawled on the large bed. Luckily, Auntie hadn't changed a bit. 'This bay window is a lovely place to sleep, too. I have lots of dreams here.'

'Then you'll probably be dreaming of Tim,' teased Auntie, and sat down next to me on the bed.

I blushed. 'No, mostly about my mother. I can almost touch her, but when I wake up, she disappears immediately.'

'That's nice. Not that she's gone when you wake up, but that you dream about her when you're asleep.' Aunt Karly got up and walked over to her suitcase. She pulled out an envelope that lay on top of her things and gave it to me.

'From Tim.'

'Tim?' I cried, and I felt all the little hairs on my arm stand up. Incredulously, I stared at the envelope in my hands.

'I'm going to see how your father's doing. We haven't seen each other for a long time, either.' Aunt Karly left the room and softly closed the door behind her.

A letter from Tim! That was the last thing I had expected. I'd hoped for one, of course. I turned the letter over carefully, smelled it and determined that the paper smelled like paper. Nothing special. Where did it come from? Where could Tim be? I took a deep breath and tore open the envelope.

A small black and white photograph fell out of the envelope. A picture of Tim. I held it in my hand and stared at it for a while. His hair was cropped, the long strands that stuck out in all directions had gone. His eyes, that I found so special with that greeny-brown colour and with the white flecks in the iris, didn't stand out on this photograph, because it was black and white. His mouth still curled up at the corners, but he looked very serious. It was Tim and at the same time, it wasn't Tim at all. I sighed and took the letter from the envelope and unfolded the sheet of paper. I found it difficult to start on the letter. I was afraid of reading things I didn't want to know at all. Such as bad news about how Tim had fared. Finally, my curiosity won. I had to know how Tim was doing.

Singapore, Wilhelmina Camp,
15 December 1945

Nell,

You've found your father. I'm happy for you. I'm glad you got out of Surabaya safely.

I'm now in Singapore in the Wilhelmina Camp.

GIRL OUT OF PLACE

According to the Red Cross, my mother was supposed to be here, but she isn't. It turned out to be a woman with the same name. I had hoped to find you here, but you had already left when I got here.

So much has happened since you last saw me, as I was being taken away by the Pemudas in an army truck. It's as if we keep just missing each other. These are strange times. At sea, there are ships full of displaced people trying to find their lost loved ones. As soon as I have transport, I'm coming to Australia. Apparently, my mother is there now. Most of all, I want to see you. What about you?

Tim Thissen

I read the letter several times. I tasted the words, weighed them up. Then I put the sheet of paper back in the envelope. My hands were trembling. I tried to form an opinion of the letter, but I was just very excited. Was I happy with his letter? Yes, I was. It gave me a warm feeling and it brought Tim back to life again a little, because sometimes I thought I had only imagined him. But what was I to make of the letter? He didn't write about what he had been through at all. It was a strange letter, but what did I know? I didn't know anything about letters from boys. I had only had a few. Tim's letter was a bit formal, but then again, it wasn't. A plain opening. There was no 'Dear Nell' or 'Hi Nell'. And a nondescript ending with just his name.

Had I expected a love letter? I hadn't, had I? What did it take for a letter to be called a love letter? Tim wrote that most of all he wanted to see me. Was that love? And what about me? What did I want? Now what kind of a question was that. Of course, I wanted to see him again! I would write to him immediately. It would be fantastic if he came to Bondi.

SYL VAN DUYN

'I'm just going to post my letter,' I said to my father and Aunt Karly, who were sitting outside on a low wall. Aunt Karly jumped up and pulled my father up, too. 'We'll walk with you. I've only got a few opportunities to go for a walk with you two. The evening is much too lovely to go in already. Come on Pete. On your feet.'

There was a letter box two blocks down in Warners Avenue. As I posted the letter, I felt elated. Of course, my letter wasn't half as long as Tim's. I wasn't much of a writer, but I had really done my best and as I put the letter into the envelope, just for a moment, I felt really close to Tim. That had seemed like a good sign, but now that I heard the letter dropping to the bottom of the letter box, I wasn't so sure anymore.

We walked down Queen Elizabeth drive for a bit to the beach. There were still lots of people out. It was a lovely evening and there were ever so many stars in the sky. We talked about insignificant things, but it was nice because Aunt Karly was there. Even my father was more talkative than usual. And tonight, among all the other people in the street, we seemed to be simply a normal family, that hadn't experienced anything special, a family that no-one would notice.

That night, in my bay window, I dreamt that Nathan and Tim were taking part in the Surf Race of the North Bondi Surf Life Saving Club. That was a competition Nathan had told me about because he wanted to take part in it next year. The participants started on the beach. They ran, waded, swam one hundred and seventy metres into the sea past some buoys, turned back to the beach and then ran to the finish that was marked with flags. In my dream, I stood with my mother at the finish line. When Nathan and Tim arrived at the finish my mother said: 'Take care, Nelly. It's not the right time yet. Those boys seem to be the same, but appearances can be deceiving.' And then my mother vanished into thin air.

When I opened my eyes, Aunt Karly was lying next to me and I couldn't help crying. Auntie put an arm around me and luckily, she didn't say anything. We lay like that for a while. Then I felt a lot better and got out of bed. 'Come on, Auntie, I'm going to show you the North Bondi Surf Life Saving Club.'

CAREFREE DAYS

'Promise that you won't be too sad when I'm gone,' said Aunt Karly. We were standing outside near the Ford, which my father had borrowed again. This time, he was going to take Auntie to the port, but I wasn't going to go along. I didn't want to. It was too hard to have to stand on the quayside and wave goodbye to her as the ship left harbour on its way to the Netherlands. I was afraid that I'd beg her to stay and that I'd make the departure difficult for her, too. I didn't want that. I wanted her to leave Bondi, where we had been so happy together, with a positive feeling, and that's why I chose to say goodbye here in front of our house. I kissed Auntie on both cheeks, and she held me tight for a moment. 'We'll see each other again soon. Carry on with your life. Agreed?'

I wriggled out of her embrace. 'Agreed. I will miss you, but I'll do my best not to be too sad.'

My father was already at the wheel. He leant out of the car window. 'I won't be gone too long, Nell. I'll drop off the car in Sydney and come home by tram. See you later.'

I nodded and raised my hand as a salute to him. Now please leave quickly, I thought. Go. If this took too long, it was going to be a tearful farewell, after all. Aunt Karly got in. I watched, but I didn't let it touch me. I just looked and listened. The slamming of car doors. The final goodbyes. The horn as a farewell salute. Screeching tyres because my father accelerated too wildly as he drove off. Typical of my father; he'd done that for as long as I could remember. When I finally looked up, the street was empty.

Slowly I went inside, went up the stairs to my room. Then I closed the window; I didn't want to hear the sea. I drew the curtains; I couldn't bear the sunlight. *Bye bye world! I'm not here anymore.* I crawled onto my bed in the bay window, pulled my knees up to my chin and wrapped my arms around them. To be as small as I could make myself. I was just a very small, lonely girl. All alone in Bondi. I just couldn't do it. Aunt Karly had to come back, to hold me tight and rock me until I fell asleep. But I had promised her not to feel sad, so I tried to think of all the lovely things that we'd done together these past few days. My father had been glad to take a back seat while I was in her company, and hadn't bothered with me so much. He never went out with us, except for the time we'd gone to Sydney when Aunt Karly needed to buy warm clothes for her trip to the Netherlands, where it was very cold now. Auntie had stayed here in Bondi for ten days, and in that time, I had been to the North Bondi Surf Life Saving Club just once, and that was to show Auntie where I spent my time.

'It's great, that you've developed into such a strong swimmer here,' said Aunt Karly, when I showed her the club. 'You were always good at that.' I thought it was funny that she remembered that, because Aunt Karly and I had only swum together once or twice.

Bondy knocked on my door and asked if I was coming for lunch. I answered that I wasn't hungry. She stood outside my door for a moment, not knowing what to do, and a little while later I heard her going downstairs. I found myself going back over things again and again. What else could I remember of the past ten days? We had walked a lot by the sea. And discussed many things. 'Now that you're back, it's as if I've found a part of myself again and feel more whole.'

Aunt Karly took my hand. 'It's the same for me. I believe that in your heart, you carry a fragment of all the people that are important to you. And all those little pieces together colour who you are.'

'So we're just what other people make of us? You don't have a say yourself?'

'Of course, you do, Nell. There is such a thing as free will. The fragments of others, that you carry with you, influence you, but which parts do that and how important they become, is largely up to you.'

'I don't understand that.'

'There's a part of you in me. At the moment, I'm walking with you by the sea. Later, in the Netherlands, of all the things we've shared, I'll choose this moment to cherish.'

'So, what you're really saying is, that you're the one who decides what you think! I don't think that's possible.'

'Not entirely, but you can steer it. I don't want to constantly think of our time in the camp, so I try to concentrate on our time here together in Bondi.'

I sighed. 'I wish that this time here with you would never end. Please stay! It's much harder to talk to my father. I think it's because I'm so similar to my mother.'

Reassuringly, Aunt Karly squeezed my hand. 'That, too. It's difficult for your father. He misses Elenore and he needs time to get over it. It's because of the war.'

'But you said that the war is in everyone.'

'Yes, that's true. It's in you, in me, in everyone who survived it. Everyone has to get used to normal life and that's why no-one is making a move. But if you stay stuck in the past, you're not really living. I want to look ahead.' That last part, especially, is what I recall her saying, and I really wanted to remember that.

Late in the evening, when it was already dark, I was suddenly awakened by my father who was knocking on my door and asking if I was alright. He was home much later than he had promised. I pretended to be asleep. I didn't want to talk to anybody. I wanted to think about Aunt Karly's words: being stuck in the past wasn't living. I didn't want to forget anything that we'd done over the past few days, either.

Aunt Karly had taught me to knit. 'A woman who can knit a scarf for her husband is ready to get married,' she quipped on the third day that she was in Bondi. 'That's what Granny always used to say. Do you remember that?'

I shook my head. 'Can you knit, Auntie?'

'Absolutely. But just imagine, Nell: knitting a scarf for your husband when you're living in a tropical climate!' She laughed. 'When would you wear something like that? Only if you're going on a trip to the Netherlands. But I'll gladly teach you.' And so, she did.

'You just measure yourself and then you knit your own length once. Then that scarf is exactly the right size. I won't ask who you're knitting that scarf for,' said Auntie, as she set up the stitches for me on a knitting needle. I looked at the knitting on my desk. Dark green wool with light brown flecks in it. When I had knitted a dozen rows, Aunt Karly had said: 'If you unravel your knitting at night, you'll be just like Penelope, when she was waiting for the return of her husband Odysseus from the war.'

'Yes,' I said, laughing. 'Do you mean the woman who promises her lovers she'll marry them when the cloth she is weaving is finished?'

'Precisely! And every night, she undoes her whole day's work.'

'I wouldn't do that. I'm glad I've finished even a small part of the scarf,' I said, merrily. 'And I'm not waiting for anyone.'

'Are you sure?'

'Maybe I'm waiting a little bit, but I'll just carry on knitting anyway.' I examined my scarf. I had knitted about fifty centimetres now. One needle one way. One needle the other way. Who would have thought that I would enjoy knitting? Not me. Millions of stitches to go and if I made a mistake, I couldn't ask Auntie to help me. *No, don't think about it.* I was simply going to finish that scarf. For Tim? I couldn't say anymore.

Only now did I realize that the conversations with Aunt Karly, here, were different to the ones we had had when we were trying to survive together in the Dutch East Indies. She had felt responsible for me then, but now she tried to talk to me as if I were a grown-up.

'You want me to look ahead. So why are you leaving for the Netherlands then, to revisit the past with your fiancé?'

'Because it's not easy to look ahead. For me, going back to Holland, is the start of me reinventing myself. That's one way of looking at it.'

'I'd like that, too, to reinvent myself,' I sighed.

'Well, I think you've already started doing that a little bit here in Bondi. Making your own choices, that's what it's all about. Giving a direction to your own life.'

'I don't know. The camp, my mother. None of that was a choice.'

'No, that was the war knocking you flat.'

'Going to Jakarta, then being sent to Bondi, they weren't my choices either.'

'No, your father decided that for you, because you're only fifteen.'

'Almost sixteen, on the 1ˢᵗ February. That's a month away.'

'But until you're eighteen, your father has parental authority over you. Which doesn't mean you can't think about what you want out of life. You need to work out what makes you smile.'

'You do, of course!' I cried, and I gave her a push and ran away along the beach until I stood knee high in the water. I spent hours going back over what we had done together, but for the time being, I wouldn't be seeing my aunt again. How could I not feel sad about that?

'You can't just shut yourself up in your room for days on end,' said my father.

We were having breakfast in the dining room downstairs. Well, I was mostly drinking tea and my father was enjoying an English breakfast of fried eggs, bacon, fried sausages and baked beans in tomato sauce. I couldn't understand how he managed to eat it all. 'Come on, Cornelia. First you hide in your room for two days and now you haven't left the house for eight days.'

There was egg yolk on his chin, and it was dripping onto his plate. His lips were greasy. 'You promised Aunt Karly not to be upset, but since she left, you haven't been out.' He wiped his mouth with his napkin, went to the calendar on the wall and looked at it quickly. 'Today is the twelfth, I have to go to Sydney. Why don't you come along with me, Cornelia? It will do you good.'

I shook my head. 'I'm going to the Life Saving Club again today.'

'Really? Will you really go or are you just saying that to humour me?'

'Of course not. I'll go. I promise!'

My father was right. I knew I couldn't go on like this, but it was hard admitting that to him. I really had to get moving. Aunt Karly had told me, 'If you stay stuck in the past, you're not living.' I'd thought about that a lot over the past few days. About how I should go about that: looking ahead, reinventing myself, and in particular, giving direction to my own life. To stay in my room was to stand still. Going to the beach, swimming and hanging out with the people at the club was a start. I had been brooding about it all, trying to work things out. I realized that I hadn't a clue about who I really was or what I would like to do in the future.

What I did know about myself, was mainly what others had told me:

That I would be sixteen years old on 1st February – that's what the calendar says.

That I have a talent for swimming – so say Nathan and Aunt Karly.

That I look like a mermaid – says Jamie.

That I have a strong body – says Nathan.

That I'm a beautiful young woman – says Aunt Karly.

That the war is in me – says Aunt Karly.

That I look just like my mother – says my father.

That people want to see me again – says Tim.

That I should think more about what I want out of life – says Aunt Karly.

My father looked at me, anxiously. 'What are you thinking, Cornelia? Are you sure, that you won't come to Sydney?'

To reassure him, I smiled at him. 'Yes, I'm sure. I think I'll go and join the North Bondi swimmers. Then I can take part in the swimming competitions against the other clubs. If that's alright with you?'

'Of course, that's alright. Anything is better than sitting here doing nothing all day.' Clearly relieved, my father got up and planted a kiss on the top of my head. 'Then I'll see you tonight. Bye Nell.'

An hour later, I was at the Life Saving Club. It was nine o'clock in the morning and it wasn't very busy yet. The first person I met was Nathan, in his swimming trunks and wearing his goggles on top of his head.

'Long time no see,' he said with a grin.

'Family obligations,' I answered with a similar grin.

'Cool that you're here. Are you coming swimming again?'

'Only if I can take part in the competitions against other swimming clubs.'

'Depends on how good you are,' teased Nathan. 'Anyway, you can always come along as a supporter. During the competitions, we can use all the help we can get. Are you coming right now?'

I looked at him questioningly. 'To do what precisely?'

'To swim, of course!'

It took a moment for me to comprehend what he was saying.

'Let me just get changed. Back in a moment.' I ran to the changing cubicles. I was going to reinvent myself.

※

'Maybe in a few weeks' time you'll be fit enough to swim for our team against the Bondi Iceberg Club,' said Nathan, a few days later. It was early on a Saturday morning, and I was going along to Tamarama Beach to support Nathan's team. 'Iceberg Club is in South Bondi and they swim at Bogey Hole, close to Bondi Baths.'

'Yes!' I cried, enthusiastically. 'When?'

'Somewhere in the middle of February. You have just under three weeks to get in shape.'

'That would be fantastic! Really great.' Enthusiastically, I put my arms around Nathan. For a second, we converged like a shadow with the beams of the sun, but when he looked into my eyes, I got confused and stepped back and just blabbered on. 'What kind of club is that, South Bondi Iceberg Club? They have such an odd name. As if there are icebergs in Bondi. We'll easily beat people who give their club such a silly name.'

'You don't understand,' said Nathan. 'It's a swimming club that was founded by people who like to swim in the winter. They are the best. But if you take part, we're bound to win this time!' He smiled. I smiled back and I felt myself almost purring with pleasure.

'Come on,' said Nathan. 'It's time. We're off.'

I had forgotten that life could be so carefree. Here I was on a Saturday morning with the girls from the North Bondi Life Saving Club, and I was shouting myself hoarse with my encouragements for our team. Yes, our team! I was part of it. My life wasn't standing still anymore. I was moving forwards at full speed. I was well on my way to becoming a real Bondi girl. And I had decided that this was what I wanted: to live in Bondi with my father and to be a carefree Bondi girl of the Bondi swimming team, in my Bondi bikini and with my Bondi boyfriend. Well, I didn't know about that last bit yet. All the girls had a boyfriend, but I wasn't sure that I wanted to be that much of a Bondi girl.

For a week now, I had been training every morning with Nathan. My swimming was getting better and better. From nine o'clock onwards, I spent most days at the beach or at the swimming club. In the evenings, I ate with my father and often we went for an evening stroll along the Campbell Parade and Ramsgate Avenue to the lookout point at the end of Ramsgate and then home again. Then I went to bed and fell straight asleep. I didn't dream anymore, or if I did dream, I couldn't remember what had preoccupied me during the night. Sometimes my father and I went beyond Ramsgate and we'd walk from the viewing point across the rocks to the beach. If we walked together, things were easier between my father and me. We didn't talk much. I didn't know what was on his mind. I didn't tell him how I was trying to give direction to my own life.

The shouting of the supporters brought me back to Tamarama Beach. North Bondi had won the away match with ease. As part of the supporters' team, I hadn't shouted myself hoarse for nothing. It was still early when we gathered at the pick-up truck that had brought us to Tamarama Beach and that would take us back again. It was a worn-out piece of junk that belonged to one of the swimmers.

The first time that I was to go with the swimming team, this pick-up had pulled up next to us, and I had thought up an excuse so that, at the very last moment, I didn't have to get in. The pick-up reminded me too much of my flight in the army truck to the harbour of Surabaya. It was a scene from my life prior to Bondi. A life that was so weird, so surreal, that I sometimes couldn't imagine it had really happened and not been just a dream. The second time, I had taken a deep breath and had got in. The pick-up truck was part of my life in Bondi now. I would just have to get used to that. Anyway, it wasn't too bad in the back. You had the feeling that you could always jump out if you needed to.

'We'll be back at two o'clock. I can do some training,' I said to Nathan. We were the only ones who hadn't got in the truck yet.

'I've got other plans. I'm going to Sydney. Want to come?'

Our eyes met for a moment. 'Yes,' said my heart, 'I'll come,' and it missed a beat. But my mind said: 'No, sorry Nathan, I'm going with the team back to Bondi.'

'It's alright to miss a day of training, Neal. You're sure to be on the team against the Iceberg Club.'

'I'm glad to hear it, but I'm not coming to Sydney.'

'Are you getting in or not?' cried Sarah, one of the girls from the North Bondi supporters' team, who was in the back of the pick-up.

I signalled her 'I'm coming,' and I jumped in the back of the truck. The doors of the cab banged shut. The engine started. Someone shouted at us from inside the driver's cab.

'Then I'll go with you,' decided Nathan. At the very last moment, he jumped in the back next to me and Sarah. Honking its horn, the truck accelerated and left the parking lot.

We drove along the coastal road back to Bondi. I had to hold on tight, otherwise I would have been flung around in the back. It was incredibly hot. Even the wind was hot. I wondered if I looked just as hot and sweaty as Sarah and Nathan.

'If this heat goes on, we'll soon have a bushfire,' said Sarah.

'You're damned right,' grunted Nathan.

'If that happens, there's nothing for it but to get into the sea,' I said.

That made Nathan and Sarah laugh. I didn't mind them making fun of me but wondered why they found my remark so amusing. In Sarah's company, I was still the girl from afar.

I knew nothing about bushfires so I'd better stay out of this conversation.

Nathan gave me a thumb's up. 'Good idea Neal, into the sea! It's lucky we're good at swimming. And so we should be. I want to be a champion swimmer anyway.'

'You're the best one on our team,' said Sarah, flirtatiously. 'Championship assured. Have you heard anything from the university yet?'

I was so surprised that I forgot my resolution to keep my mouth shut. 'Do you want to go to university? Won't you have to give up on being a swimming champion then?' I asked, surprised.

'If I swim in a team that wins the championship and I swim a personal best, I can go to a university that wants me in the swimming team and I'll get a scholarship. And I do want to go to university. Civil engineering. I want to learn how to build awesome bridges like the Sydney Harbour Bridge.'

'I'm sure you'll get a scholarship,' I said softly. I didn't know things worked like that and I felt stupid. I thought swimming was a goal, but for Nathan, it was a means. That confused me. I kept quiet and watched the road.

Just before we reached the North Bondi Life Saving Club, I saw my father walking down Queen Elizabeth Drive. He was walking with the woman he had borrowed the car from. Wendy from the airbase. He had his arm around her shoulders, and they were close together. In that instant, I felt very light in my head and also a bit sick. I ducked down in the back of the truck. I didn't want him to see me. Luckily, my father just carried on walking and as he had eyes only for Wendy, I needn't have worried.

Nathan put his hand on my arm. 'Are you alright? You've gone pale.'

I pulled myself together. I didn't want to tell him what I

had just seen. If I didn't say anything about it, I could pretend it hadn't happened. I wanted things to be carefree. 'It's nothing,' I said, as the truck stopped in front of the club. 'It's the heat.'

'Sorry guys, I promised to be home around now,' said Sarah, as she gathered her things and jumped down from the back. 'See you next time, Nathan.' She blew him a kiss and walked in the direction of the boulevard. Admiringly, I watched how she did it. No, I wasn't a Bondi girl by a long stretch yet: that much was clear.

'Do you still want to go for a swim?' asked Nathan, when we had got out and the pick-up truck had driven off.

I nodded. 'I do. I'm no way good enough yet, and you need to improve on your personal best, don't you?'

A few moments later, we were heading for the water with a few more fanatical swimmers. Nathan walked next to me. 'Why didn't you want to come to Sydney with me, Neal?'

I smiled but said nothing.

'Why is that funny?'

'The way you say my name. That's funny. Neal instead of Nell.'

'Is it short for something?'

'Nell is from the Dutch Cornelia. My granny's name.'

'Well that's alright then, Neal from Cornelia.'

I gave up. 'Were you named after anyone?'

Nathan shrugged. 'Of course. I was named after my father and he was named after his father and he was named after his father. And so on.'

'You're the first Nathan I've met.'

'I'm the youngest Nathan in the family. Nathan: it means gift of god. My parents are from Poland and they're Jewish. Luckily, they emigrated to Australia in the mid-1930s. I was five. No-one survived from my family back in Poland.'

'I'm so sorry.'

'That's okay. I didn't know them, those Polish family members. I'm still connected to them, because they're blood relatives, but I never met them, and I can't remember anything about my Polish childhood.' Nathan ran to the sea and dived into the water. 'One hundred metre sprint!' And away he went.

I pressed the stopwatch and timed him. I was surprised that Nathan was less of a Bondi boy than I had assumed. I thought he was from one of those families that had lived in Australia forever. I didn't understand why Nathan was being so offhand about the fate of his family. I checked Nathan's time, before handing him the stopwatch. '60.01, not bad.'

'My goal is 59.01.' Nathan pointed at the sea. 'Now you, Neal. Go for it.'

Quickly, I grabbed back the stopwatch. 'First I want to know why you're acting so tough about your family.'

'I'm not acting tough. For me, now, then, and later is a single entity, and in that way, I stay connected with people who aren't here anymore and who I've never met.' Nathan was serious now.

I raised my eyebrows. I thought of my mother and how I dreamt of her. I thought of my father, who had apparently connected with Wendy. But Nathan probably meant something else. 'How then? How do you stay connected?'

Nathan took the stopwatch from my hand again. 'I'll tell you later. Training first. One thousand metres for you.'

After the training, Nathan walked me to Warners Avenue. He wanted to see where I lived. He didn't even need to take a detour because he lived fifteen minutes further on up in Bondi. It was still incredibly hot and once I was dry, the heat clung to me like a hot blanket. I was curious about Nathan's ideas about how people who weren't here anymore still stayed connected. It hadn't been out of my thoughts at all during training. 'Tell me,' I said, 'How do you see that connection between people?'

'It's very simple. The past and the future together form a whole because the spirits of our forefathers stay present in everything and connect everything with each other. Aboriginals believe that. They were the first inhabitants of Australia. For them, there's a dreamtime: a time from before such a thing as time existed. A time before the world was created. Because of that dreamtime, everything is connected: the sun, moon, stars, trees, mountains, rivers, the people and the animals.'

'Now, then and later.'

'You've got it!'

'Maybe.'

Because of our conversation, we had hardly noticed that we were already in front of my house.

'I'm home,' I said.

'Neal, I believe that, too, that everything is connected. People, animals, you and me.'

My heart pounded in my chest. Nathan's face was very close. He took my face in his hands and before I realized it, we were kissing. First, very gently and carefully. Then more and more intensely, almost fiercely. I left the ground and floated across the earth. Nathan tasted of the sea: of course he did. I knew nothing about kissing, but now I leant close to Nathan and it happened of its own accord.

But suddenly I saw myself standing with Nathan in front of the house at Warners Avenue. I wondered what in heaven's name I was doing there. I was ashamed of myself. I wanted to get away from there. In that moment, I didn't want to be with Nathan at all anymore.

'See you tomorrow,' I said, and fled inside.

TOO BAD

'I need to talk to you,' announced my father on Sunday morning. He entered my room – something he normally never did – and sat down in the only chair. He had to fold his legs to be able to sit in that wobbly wicker thing. In order to strike a pose, he had crossed his arms in front of his chest. He looked uncomfortable, my tall father squeezed into a small wicker chair, and it didn't bode well.

I was still in bed and I had hardly slept that night. I had been too excited. My lips tingled whenever I thought of Nathan. And the fact that I had let him kiss me. Perhaps I shouldn't have done that. Could you be friends and train together and at the same time share something other than friendship? Back in the camp, I had dreamed of kissing a boy and now I had kissed two. No, that wasn't true. Nathan had kissed me. Jamie hadn't, but his lips had brushed mine. The kiss of a mermaid. I had imagined the rest: or at least, that's what I thought. It was all very confusing. What was I afraid of? It was a journey across the stars, or rather, it was as if I was on a roller coaster when I kissed Nathan. So why had I run away? Was it because of Tim? I didn't know. I would probably never see Tim again. I'd left Jakarta a long time ago, and except for the letter that Aunt Karly had brought me, I hadn't heard anything from him.

When I had rushed in last night, my father had been waiting in the kitchen.

'At last, there you are,' he said. He looked at me the way he always did when he wanted to make me feel really small. 'Are you getting enough sleep?' Then he got up and left the room without saying anything. He had been out himself with that Wendy, of course, and now he was being difficult about me. I had stayed in the kitchen for a bit. Just stood there and looked at myself in the mirror of the sideboard. I looked just the same as usual. Even if I had reinvented myself by kissing Nathan so wildly, there was nothing to show for it. I put my mouth on the mouth of my reflection and tried to establish what I looked like when I was kissing someone. The mirror immediately fogged up. With my finger, I drew a little heart on the steamed-up glass of the mirror. After that, I had crept very quietly to my room and had lain awake all night in my bay window.

'I need to talk to you,' my father repeated.

I looked at him sleepily. 'Now? Can't it wait?'

'No, I want to talk to you now.'

'Alright.' I sat up in bed. 'I'm sorry I was home so late last night. I went to Tamarama with the people from the swimming club and after that, we did some training.'

'It's not just about last night, Cornelia. You're running wild here. You do nothing but hang around at the beach with those local kids. You're flirting.'

I looked crossly at my father. How would he know if I was flirting or not, as he'd never seen me with anyone from the club? Well, not since the first day when he'd spoken to Nathan. 'You're the one who's flirting,' I wanted to say. 'I saw you yesterday with that Wendy and she's only a few years older than I am.' But I didn't dare to, and so instead I said: 'I'm not hanging around at the beach. I'm training to take part in the swimming matches of the North Bondi Life Saving Club.'

'And you hang around with those local kids.'

'They're my friends! You wanted me to go and do something and not sit moping in my room. And you were happy with me going swimming, training! I asked you!'

'I didn't realize what the consequences would be.'

'What consequences? I'm finally young again. I'm swimming. I'm laughing. I've got a life again. Is that not allowed?'

'Of course, it is. But I think it's time you went to school!'

'Boarding school, I suppose?' I said, as a joke.

'Exactly! Boarding school seems like a really good option to me!'

Boarding school! He really meant it. The walls of the room spun, and I could see my father floating through space. I took a deep breath, and everything dropped back in place. I looked at him incredulously. 'You can't be serious?'

'I'm not joking, Cornelia. You can't spend the rest of your life playing around outdoors.'

The room spun again. 'What is wrong with that?' I shouted, angrily. 'What is wrong with that? I can't spend the rest of my life feeling sorry for myself about everything that has happened. At last I have a normal life again with a house, a father and friends and now you want to take me away from here! You can't just do that!'

My father just carried on talking without raising his voice, as if I hadn't blown up at him. If I had left the room, he would have carried on talking to the empty bed.

'I've looked at a few schools. The Morongo Girls College

in Geelong seems like a very suitable school for you.'

'Please, don't just send me away like that,' I begged, panicking.

'Either way, we're going to have a look at that school. There's nothing wrong with that. Tomorrow morning we're going over there to get acquainted. So, put on something nice tomorrow.' With some difficulty, my father got up from the little wicker chair and left the room. At the door, he turned around. 'We leave at eight o'clock.'

I couldn't believe what had just happened. In disbelief, I stared at the chair where my father had been sitting as he said all those awful things. Would he really send me to boarding school?

I didn't want to think about it. I jumped out of bed. I didn't want to stay at home. My father could come up with whatever plan he liked. Aunt Karly said I had to focus on what I wanted. I was going to swim as usual. I felt like going for a really long swim. I grabbed my swimming gear and put it into my bathing bag. I shut the door to my room and pounded down the stairs.

I wasn't going to go. That was my first thought when I woke up on Monday morning. I had no interest in this day, I would just stay in bed. Yesterday, I had trained really hard for the one thousand metre freestyle and then I had stayed at the beach for a long time. When everyone had gone home, I'd walked with Nathan by the shore. We had talked and kissed. Kissed for a long time as the water ran across our feet. It gave me goose bumps all over, but it also confused me. I still didn't know what to think. I thought Tim was more my kind, but

I was making out with Nathan. We sat really close together, talking about all sorts of things, including my father.

'He wants to send me to boarding school. In Geelong.'

'When?' asked Nathan. 'Surely, not now?'

'As soon as possible. He thinks I'm running wild here.'

Nathan looked at me searchingly. 'Seriously?'

I nodded. 'Tomorrow, we're going to have a look.'

'That's a long trip. Geelong is further than Melbourne.'

'We're flying,' I said. 'But if Geelong is further than Melbourne, how far is it then from Bondi Beach?'

'At least one thousand kilometres.'

'That far!' I was furious when I realized what my father's plan entailed. 'I don't want to be banished to the outback of Australia and I don't feel like walking here beside the sea anymore. I'm going home!'

'I don't understand you,' said Nathan. 'You're not leaving Bondi yet, and you're acting like you've already left. We've still got time enough together.'

'There's no point being with you if I know that I'm never going to see you again.'

'You don't know that.' Nathan was standing behind me with his hands on my stomach and was kissing my neck. 'Come on, stay!' He drew me closer.

I pulled away. 'No, I want to go home.'

'I'll walk you.'

'You don't need to. I'd prefer to go alone before I have another fight with my father.' I blew him a hand kiss and before Nathan could answer, I ran away across the beach. Not that I was really worried about arguing with my father, but I did want to be alone. When I got back, the house was empty. I stormed upstairs to my room and banged the door shut behind me.

No, I simply wasn't going there. I refused to. I couldn't and I wouldn't. Today, I was going to stay here in my room, I was definitely *not* going to board that plane, and I was *not* going to look at that stupid boarding school. That's what I thought, but of course, it didn't work out that way. I didn't dare oppose my father and perhaps I was also a teeny bit curious about what he had in mind for me. So, I had to get up.

'Put on a nice dress,' was what my father had ordered last night. I looked in the closet and let my dresses slide through my hands. There was the dress with the polka dots, that I had made with Aunt Karly. I had to write to her that my father had gone mad and wanted to send me to boarding school. I bet she didn't know about that! If she had been here, my father would never have dared do such a thing. Aunt Karly would never have permitted it. The white silk dress with the coloured ribbons from the safe house in De Wijk. Aunt Karly had said that dress looked really good on me, especially now I was so tanned. But I didn't feel like wearing a party dress on a day like this. No way! I refused to do that. To annoy my father, I put on the military clothes he had brought from Manila.

When I walked into the dining room for breakfast, my father was already sitting at the table. He was wearing his aviation uniform. 'Good morning, Cornelia,' he said, in a friendly way. Of course, he was once again pretending that nothing had occurred yesterday. He looked at me and absorbed my military khaki trousers and my khaki shirt, impassively. 'Nice dress,' he said, slightly mockingly.

'Thank you,' I said as coolly as I could, but it took an effort to stay calm. I poured my tea and stayed silent, seething.

My father had arranged for us to fly with Captain Somers by military plane from Sydney to Geelong.

'Nice to see you again,' Somers greeted me in a friendly way.

I thought of Jamie and felt the blood rushing to my cheeks. Did Somers know about that nocturnal swim?

'You look well,' said Somers. 'Life in Bondi must have done you good.'

'Not everyone thinks that,' I said, and looked challengingly at my father. He pretended he hadn't heard and sat next to Somers in the co-pilot's seat. He directed me to a spot at the back of the cockpit. As soon as I had fastened my seatbelt, the plane picked up speed and lifted off. Soon, we had reached a great height and when I looked out, all I could see was the sky. Heaven must be close. Flying was perhaps the most beautiful thing there was. 'I think I want to be a pilot, too,' I said.

My father almost choked because it made him laugh and he was trying not to.

'I'm serious,' I said angrily. 'It's nothing to laugh about.' I could see that Somers was following our conversation, but he didn't join in.

'I'm not laughing,' answered my father, 'I choked.'

'Because you were laughing.'

My father sighed. 'If you want to be a pilot, you will have to finish secondary school. As far as that is concerned, Morongo Girls College is your best bet. But believe me, you're better off choosing another profession.'

'There are lots of women who flew Spitfires during the war and made a very good job of it. You know that.'

'That was different. That was war. Flying is not for girls. They've just opened a new National Aviation School in the Netherlands, and they don't accept girls.'

I sighed and looked out of the window at the cloud cover. Another reason not to want to go to school.

'I'm not going to go there,' I said to my father, when we finally got home late in the evening of the next day, and the two of us were alone again. 'I'll die if you leave me there.' I threw the school uniform that my father had bought for me in Geelong into my closet.

'You'll need that uniform when you go to school,' my father said, very calmly, 'and I paid a lot of money for it.'

'You shouldn't have bothered. I'm not going somewhere where I have to wear a uniform. People with uniforms are warmongers.'

'The war is over,' said my father.

'That war started because people wore uniforms. If they hadn't done that, history would have run a very different course. If you wear a uniform, you take leave of your own free will and you do what other people want you to do.'

'Where on earth did you get that nonsense from? I wear a uniform, too.'

'Yes, and where did it get you? I'm not going to Geelong. I want to stay in Bondi. I'm happy here.'

'Come on, Nell, this is a half-way point here, we have to move on. I have to get back to work and my work is in Jakarta. That's no place for you. You saw that for yourself. Be reasonable.'

'Stay here then! My mother would never have sent me to boarding school!'

'Too bad. Your mother is dead!' shouted my father.

'Yes, I'm really upset that she's dead, but it doesn't bother you because you've already got another girlfriend!' I screamed back.

My father turned red with rage. 'You're starting at that school on 2nd February. That's final!'

I hadn't dreamt of my mother for a long time, but tonight I was walking together with her through high grass along the paddy fields. It smelt like only the Indies smell; of spices, nuts, flowers all covered in a damp mist. We were walking barefoot and both wearing the same blue sarong. Suddenly, my mother disappeared. I walked on. My mother whispered: 'I can hear the rustling of your sarong in the high grass. I will always be with you. In time, before time. You're stronger than you think. Time heals.' I walked between the paddy fields and searched everywhere for my mother, but found only that whispering voice, that passed into the rustling of the grass.

I woke up confused from that dream, and it left me feeling uneasy. As if I had forgotten to do something really important, that would have warded off disaster, without knowing what. I wrote Aunt Karly an airmail letter.

Dear Aunt Karly,

If only you were here. If only you had never gone to Holland. Another eleven days and I'll be deported from the Bondi paradise. This time not to a camp, but to boarding school in Geelong. My father is going back to Jakarta with his girlfriend Wendy.

I am frantic and don't know what to do. What am I supposed to do at boarding school? I don't want that at all. My father won't see reason. I don't understand. What is wrong with him? Could you talk to him?

I'd probably already have left by the time she sent an answer. *Don't think about it.* I ran down the stairs. 'I'll be at the beach.'

'Have fun,' said Bondy.

During the days I still had left in Bondi, I escaped from the house. I hardly saw my father.

'Will you walk with me to the lookout point?' he asked, during one of the few times we had dinner together.

'I want to write Auntie a letter,' I answered, evasively.

He shrugged. 'Alright.'

For the last few days, I'd been spending all my time at the club. I was a committed Bondi girl, but it didn't make me happy anymore. It was clear to me now that swimming was a means and not an end. I didn't see much of Nathan.

'Something wrong?' he asked.

'Too much stuff going on.'

'It's as if you've already left.'

I shrugged. I couldn't understand why I was acting like that, either. I was mad about Nathan, but it was too confusing to make out with him. When I kissed him, I almost always thought of Tim, and at the same time, I didn't even know if I would ever see Tim again.

The more we trained together, the more things between Nathan and me got back to normal. And we trained hard.

'You're swimming well,' Nathan had said last Monday. 'I'm sure you'll be selected for that match against the Iceberg Club.'

I clapped my hands. 'Great!' I wanted to believe that I'd still be here in the middle of February, too.

SYL VAN DUYN

It was my birthday on 1st February, the thirty-second day of the year. This year, 1st February was the first Saturday of the month. The morning of my birthday, the door to my room opened and my father came in. 'I brought you breakfast.'

He set the tray down on the floor and sat on a corner of the bed. 'Happy sixteenth birthday, dear Nell. Shall we stop being angry at each other?' He gave me a kiss. 'Shall we go out to dinner tonight together?'

'Alright,' I whimpered, and with the palm of my hand I wiped the tears away. I wasn't angry anymore. I was beaten.

'I've brought you some cinnamon cake,' said my father.

As a child, I had always been mad about it, and every year, I had it as my birthday cake. I smiled through my tears.

Late that afternoon, I went to the beach. Nathan wasn't there. Fanatically, I swam my laps. My final laps. *Don't think about it.* I hadn't told Nathan that I would be leaving for Geelong the very next day. I lingered before going home. I wasn't looking forward to going out to dinner with my father and hung around for a long time at the club. I wanted to absorb everything one last time, because I might never see it again. Deep in thought, I was standing leaning against a wall, when I heard Nathan's voice: 'There's a visitor for you!'

When I looked up, I saw Nathan's smiling face and next to him was Tim. I just couldn't believe my eyes. My head spun as if I had stayed on the merry-go-round too long. The beach, the sea and the sky seemed to keep changing position.

'Tim! What are you doing here?' I looked at him in amazement. I just couldn't understand where he'd suddenly come from. I didn't know what to think.

'I swam over!' said Tim. 'That must appeal to you because I heard you're the new Bondi swimming star.'

'Says who?'

'Says your friend Nathan.'

I must have given Tim a very blank look, because straight away he said: 'I sailed on a freighter from Singapore to Australia, and then in Sydney, I got a lift here. I was round at your place and a lady sent me to the beach.'

'That's where I met him,' added Nathan, 'and I thought I'd find you here.'

'I'm glad I made it in time for your birthday. Many happy returns.' Tim took hold of my shoulders and gave me a kiss that was lost in my hair.

'How do you know it's my birthday today?'

'Your aunt told me when she left Camp Wilhelmina for Australia. Is something the matter? You're not saying anything!'

'Sorry... I'm fine,' I said, and hugged Tim. 'Thanks for your birthday wishes. I'm glad you're here. I just didn't expect I'd ever see you again.'

'I promised you that I'd come, and then I wrote to tell you, too.'

'But you didn't come, so I thought it wasn't going to happen anymore.'

'I had to wait for a berth on a ship.'

I smiled at Tim. He looked better than in the photograph he'd sent me at Christmas. His hair was a bit longer now. 'I'm so glad you're here.'

'Good!' His eyes twinkled, just like the first time we met. It just didn't affect me in the same way when he looked at me. And it felt odd to be standing here between Nathan and Tim on Bondi beach. They didn't even know each other!

'I swim with Nathan for the North Bondi swim team,'

I said to Tim. And to Nathan I said, 'I know Tim from the Indies. We went through a lot together during the war.' Tim smiled at me when I said that, and it was only then that I realized we hadn't really experienced anything together at all.

We had only taken the same train journey. Tim was the first person I had talked to about the war and about what would come after. When I realized that, my stomach cramped. There I was, standing between two boys who really confused me.

'I didn't know it was your birthday, Neal,' said Nathan. 'She should have told me. Congratulations! You're sixteen now, aren't you?' He kissed me twice on my cheek and once on my mouth. I could feel him stiffening when I didn't kiss him back.

I blushed even more then. 'Thank you, Nathan. That's right, I'm sixteen now. I didn't tell you because I didn't want it to be my birthday.'

'That's not a crime. I'm glad you two have found each other again. I'm sure you've got a lot to talk about. See you tomorrow at training, Neal.' And with that, Nathan was gone. I had wanted to tell him that I wouldn't be coming the next day. That I wouldn't be coming ever again. But it was too late now. And I could have told him it was my birthday today. I had needlessly offended him. I hadn't meant to do that at all. I looked at Tim.

'You should have come before,' I grumbled. 'Now it's too late.' It wasn't fair to blame him. I was angry at my father and was taking it out on Tim, but Tim took it seriously.

'I wanted to, Nell, but this was the first available berth on a ship.'

'But it's too late. My father is sending me to boarding school. Tomorrow, I'm going to be interned again.'

Tim almost exploded. 'Don't say that ever again, that you're being interned!' he shouted furiously, his voice breaking. 'A boarding school isn't the same as a camp and you know it!'

'You're right. I shouldn't have said that. Not in that way'.

'So, don't say it. Your father just wants you to graduate. That's not so strange, is it? I wish my father could send me to school!'

I shrugged. 'Perhaps my father means well, but it's still ridiculous to send me to Geelong. Do you know how far that is from here?' I thought Tim was being really annoying. Not at all like the boy I remembered. I didn't need another father! With my back against the wall, I slid down to the ground until I was sitting in the sand. The sand was still warm. Tears streamed down my face. Tim sat down next to me. 'Must you really go away so soon?'

I nodded and swallowed my tears.

'I would love to come with you, Nell, but first I must find out if my mother is here in Sydney. I promised my sisters. As soon as I've done that, I'll come and see you in Geelong. I promise! Really!'

'Alright,' I said, but I didn't believe Tim would come. I didn't believe anything anymore. And if he did come, it wouldn't make any difference. I had already lost everything. I saw that Tim was looking at me. He had little lights in his eyes. 'What is the height of patience, Nell?'

'I know that one.'

'No, this one is different. The height of patience is standing on your head and then waiting for your socks to slip down.'

'Funny, but the one about the fish was better.' I smiled, wanly.

'We haven't seen each other for a long time,' said Tim.

Perhaps too long a time, I wanted to say, but I didn't. I wanted to ask Tim what had happened to him after he had been taken away by the *Pemudas* and how he had eventually reached Camp Wilhelmina, but I didn't dare. I reached for the cord around my neck and took it off. I held the ring in my hand. The gold felt cool and smooth. I showed it to Tim. 'That's yours. I found it on the floor of the train to Surabaya.'

Tim examined the ring and rubbed it between his fingers. 'The ring my father told me to give to my mother. You wrote to tell me, but it seemed too good to be true.'

'When I was getting off the train. I saw a small box lying in a corner on the floor of the carriage. I recognized it immediately, and when I opened it, there was the ring that you had shown me. But you were nowhere to be seen.'

'I'd gone off immediately to the house where my sisters were.'

'I asked everyone, and I searched everywhere for you, but you had vanished without a trace. When we had to flee Surabaya, I put the ring on a cord and wore it round my neck so I wouldn't lose it.'

'I don't know what to say. This is great, Nell. I hope I can get it to my mother.'

'Put it round your neck, then you won't lose it again.'

Without saying anything, Tim put the cord over his head. He took the ring in his hands and wanted to say something, but the only thing that came out were smothered sobs. In silence, I sat beside him and held his hand.

I'd imagined this reunion in a happier light. The grief that hung over us both was upsetting. I was sixteen years old, and was finally sitting with Tim on the beach, realizing that he was more troubled than Nathan. Tomorrow, my father would send me to a girls' school over a thousand miles away.

I couldn't help thinking that I'd never see Tim again.

TO SYDNEY

'Long time no see, Nell,' said Captain Somers when he picked me up with his car at the Morongo Girls College in Geelong. 'How long has it been?'

'Almost two years.' I shook his hand.

'How do you know that so precisely?'

I flung my blue, checked travel bag over my shoulder. 'That's easy. On 2nd February 1946, the day after my birthday, my father sent me here to boarding school. That's almost two years ago.'

'How have you been?'

'Fine!'

Somers pointed at my travel bag. 'Is that all you're taking?'

I nodded. 'I'm only staying a week. I don't need much. I can't wait to get away from here, to fly back to Sydney with you and to celebrate Christmas with my father.'

'I can imagine, but I couldn't pick you up earlier than six in the morning here.'

'Last year, I spent Christmas in Geelong. My father preferred to celebrate last Christmas with his girlfriend, Wendy.'

'That can't have been easy.'

'It was alright.' I didn't tell him that last year I'd spent most of the time in bed, crying, feeling homesick for the lovely Christmas I'd had in Bondi with Aunt Karly and my father, when life was still good. I hated that Wendy Wagner. She was seventeen years younger than my father and she didn't want me living at home. She had taken my place. *Don't think about it.* 'There are worse things,' I said cheerfully. 'But one Christmas at boarding school is enough.'

'Anyway, this year you'll be spending Christmas with your father,' said Somers. 'There's nothing like family at Christmas. So, let's get started.'

Somers walked to the car, threw my bag in the boot, and opened the passenger door. 'Come on, get in. That plane isn't going to wait for us.'

I hopped in and slammed the car door. I'd hardly settled into the seat when we were already on our way to the airport. I looked out of the window and enjoyed myself. It was still early, and everything still had to come alive, but I was ready to leave.

'So, you're going to celebrate Christmas in Jakarta?' asked Captain Somers.

'I would have preferred to have gone back to Bondi.'

'Now that would have been something, then I'd have got to see Peter again, too. I corresponded with your father to organise this flight for you, but I haven't spoken to him for a while now. How is he?'

'No idea. I haven't seen him for almost two years now since he sent me to school in Geelong. He writes to me.'

'Well, then it's about time you two got together again. Your father organized your journey himself.'

'That's no surprise,' I said, with a grin. My father liked to keep everything under control.

'Today, I'm flying you to Sydney, then you'll spend the night with my wife and I, and tomorrow, I'll put you on the train to Brisbane. From there, you take the boat to Jakarta and you'll arrive on 24th December. It's quite a trip, but you'll be with your father on Christmas Eve.'

The airfield looked deserted. The day still had to begin here, too. I could smell the aircraft fuel. I liked that smell. It reminded me of the trip with my mother and father across America, of a time when everything was still alright. I walked with Somers across the tarmac to his plane. He took enormous strides, so I had to almost run to keep up with him.

'Am I walking too fast?'

'It's alright.'

'My plane is the first to leave this morning. That's why I'm in a hurry.' He slowed down a little, 'but I can see we're on time.'

'Is it still the same old crate? The same bomber?'

'Absolutely. There's nothing like a B-25. Before you know it, we'll be in Sydney.'

'I've got a date later on in Sydney with someone I haven't seen for a long time.' I kept it vague and didn't give any details. To say as little as possible to as few people as possible was the best strategy. The less people interfered, the more you could do your own thing. So, I didn't tell Captain Somers that I had arranged to meet Tim in Sydney. If I didn't tell him, he couldn't forbid it.

'When we land in Sydney later on, I'll go straight to my appointment and I'll come round to your house tonight.'

We were standing in front of the plane. Somers stopped and took a ten-dollar bill from his trouser pocket and gave it to me. 'You're taking a taxi, understood? That way, I can be sure

I'll be able to put you safely on the train to Brisbane tomorrow. I promised your father that!'

I nodded, overwhelmed. I had expected all kinds of things, but not this. He didn't ask any questions and was fine with me going to see someone in Sydney.

'You've got my address?'

I nodded again, speechless. How could such a nice man be friends with my father?

'Good. Then let's get in.'

I sat down at the back of the cockpit. Somers took his seat at the joystick, next to the co-pilot. He turned all kinds of switches and pulled levers to get the aircraft ready for take-off.

'We're waiting for air traffic control,' said Somers. He turned towards me.

'Do you still want to be a pilot or has your father managed to put you off?'

I shrugged. 'Maybe.' I hadn't thought much more about what I wanted to do. I was in survival mode.

'Don't let him put you off. You're almost eighteen. You should follow your own path.'

My eyebrows shot up. This man was full of surprises.

'There are female pilots who've done wonderful things too. Like that Amelia Earhart with her intercontinental solo return flight. She's a cracker. She didn't let anyone stop her. She got her pilot's licence and bought her own plane.'

'Which she crashed during her flight around the world.'

'So what? She was doing what she wanted to do. You can learn something from that.'

Air traffic control called us up. Somers turned back and concentrated on the instrument panel. 'Ready for take-off.' The plane taxied slowly to the runway.

THE GARDEN OF EDEN

When I arrived at Circular Quay there was no sign of Tim. We had arranged to meet at two o'clock, near the dock of the ferry to Taronga Zoo. I looked at the boats going to and fro, at the hustle and bustle at the quayside, and I thought about Tim. I was really looking forward to seeing him again, although I couldn't say exactly why. I wasn't in love with him anymore, but he was very dear to me.

As he had promised on the beach at Bondi, Tim had visited me in Geelong. I had only just got there when he first came to see me, and that visit was engraved in my memory. I thought of all those months that I'd been longing to see him and had been looking for him desperately. And then, unannounced, he had popped up on my birthday two years ago, and I had kind of found him. But when at last he was standing right in front of me in Geelong, I didn't feel any connection with him at all. He looked like a ghost.

'I found my mother,' he said.

'Oh, I'm pleased for you.' I didn't know what else to say.

'Yes, me too,' he answered, 'because she was dead the next day. Heart attack. So, I was just in time. At least she got to see me.

But she shouldn't have died.' He kicked a closet door, which banged open.

'That's terrible! Really awful.' I shut the closet door and searched for some comforting words. I thought of what Nathan had told me once about unity in time and about how this thought, that someone who had died was never completely gone, had helped me.

'Maybe you can find your mother again in dreamtime, in the time before time. Aboriginals think that's possible and I think it's a lovely thought, that my mother might be there somewhere in that time. We meet each other often because I dream about her a lot.'

'What a load of nonsense,' said Tim. 'I don't believe in that rubbish. My mother has gone, and now I can't tell her about what happened to me in that stupid war. She just shouldn't have died.' Again, he kicked at the closet door. From a nice young man, Tim had changed into an angry young man.

'Do you know that on the day I was snatched from the street, I ended up with one hundred and twenty-five prisoners in a cell meant for twenty-five men? The *Pemudas*, armed with spears, sticks and swords, formed an archway that all the prisoners had to pass through while they hacked away at us.'

'You survived, that's what's most important!'

'You're not listening. I came to Geelong, because I thought you'd understand what I've been through, but you don't want to hear it.'

'I'm trying my best,' I said, but he was right. I wanted to shake off the war and look ahead as Auntie had advised me.

'What will you do now? Do you have any plans?'

'Don't know. Back to Sydney. I'll write to you.'

Tim left then but he did send me a letter every week. He wrote the war out of his system and in the replies I sent him,

I vented my anger at my banishment to Geelong. Tim became my distant King Kong. We didn't see each other, but we wrote. He saved me from the jungle of Geelong and we became good friends. It was just never as special between us again as that night on the train to Surabaya.

Across the quay, I could see him striding towards me.

'I'm so glad we could meet today!' Tim gave me two noisy kisses.

I responded by tousling his hair, so that it stuck up again in all directions, like when I'd first met him in another life.

'Yes, so am I. It's such a long time ago since we saw each other.'

'You can say that again, Nell. Almost two years ago in Geelong. It's a shame that you're leaving Sydney again tomorrow. It's as if your father seems to know when we're going to see each other.'

'How come? I don't get it.'

'Well, when I had finally found you last time in Bondi, your father sent you to Geelong the very next day. Now we get to see each other in Sydney and tomorrow you're being put on the boat to Jakarta! Every time we meet each other, your father sends you somewhere else.'

I shrugged. I just wanted to enjoy this day with Tim and not bother about the actions of my father. 'But now I'm here, and I've got the whole afternoon.' I told him about Somers and the taxi.

'Good man.'

'Do we have a plan?' I asked.

'Certainly,' was Tim's answer. 'I want to show you something. It's that way.' We walked along Circular Quay. At a booth, Tim bought soda water and a piece of Kraft cheese.

We drank the soda water straight away. We watched the ferries leaving for destinations with beautiful names, such as Taronga Zoo, Cockatoo Island and Watson's Bay, and ate the Kraft cheese. It felt like a tremendous luxury, a piece of that cheese in your mouth. Like something you weren't really supposed to have. Tim pointed to a big bridge that we could see clearly from the quayside. 'Harbour Bridge, isn't it beautiful? You and I were two years old when that bridge was built. They started at the two ends and built up towards the middle. Just imagine how many people worked on it, and so high above the water.'

I thought of Nathan. He wanted to be a civil engineer and build bridges just like this one in Sydney. I had heard that he had got the scholarship he wanted so much. What would he be doing now? I focused more closely on the bridge, and still I saw just a bridge. A very big bridge. I was surprised how enthusiastic Tim was about it. It was probably a guy thing, such a passion for a steel construction. We walked on along the quay and went into the Royal Botanic Gardens.

'I've never been here before,' I said.

'Good,' answered Tim. 'You'll enjoy it all the more because then everything will be new. This is my favourite place in Sydney. I come here often to think about an assignment. Usually, it results in a good idea.'

'So, you like it at the advertising agency?'

'A lot. It doesn't matter what your story is, as long as you perform well. I like that, and because I'm doing well, I'm getting better and better assignments.'

'Good.' I smiled at Tim. It was lovely to see how well he was, and I soaked up his enthusiasm. Tim smiled back and for a moment, he looked at me just like that first time we met. That confused me. I stopped.

'Wait, just taking off my sneakers.' Barefoot, I walked on across the grass. Today was the 18th December. After almost two years, I was back in Sydney and now I was walking like Eve barefoot in the Garden of Eden. It smelled lovely here. Sweet and spicy. The landscaping of the garden was breathtaking. It was just as if the exotic trees we walked past had been there for ever. Without saying much, we walked along the coastal path from Sydney harbour to the big ponds in the middle of the botanical garden.

At the biggest pond, I flopped down on the grass. We had walked for more than two hours and the grass felt like a heavenly mattress. I spread my arms out wide and stretched my legs out too. Tim lay beside me on the grass and did exactly the same. His fingertips just touched mine. It was as if tiny electric shocks travelled through my fingers to my arms and I felt funny tingles in my stomach. I thought Tim was just a good friend, but this confused me. Drops of sweat ran from my temples down the side of my head. 'I feel like jumping into the pond,' I sighed. 'And then disappearing right under the water. It's so incredibly hot.'

'I wouldn't do that. You'll be sent straight to Sydney Police station,' said Tim. 'Just lie still until you've cooled down a bit.' We looked at the bright blue sky above us and at the trees that towered over us.

'Do you see that tree, the second from the left?' asked Tim. 'The green is just a little bit different from the surrounding trees. I wanted to show you that tree. That's the Nell-and-Me-Pine. A very rare type.'

'Really?'

'Absolutely. No, just kidding. I was just being silly. There's a Wollemi Pine in this botanical garden, but it's further on among the rare and endangered species. But I made the Nell-and-Me-Pine up, I must admit. I often come here and then I look at that Nell-and-Me-Pine.'

It was only now that the name of the tree really hit me,

and my heart jumped. I could have kissed Tim, but I didn't dare. 'I didn't know you were interested in trees.'

'You can trust trees. That's why I like to walk here in the botanical gardens.' Tim got up, took my hands, and pulled me up. We stood facing each other. Tim laced his fingers through mine. He leant forward slightly, and our foreheads were touching. He looked at me intensely then kissed me gently on the mouth. I took a step back and looked at him shyly. I felt myself floating above the ground, hesitated for a moment, then put my arms around his neck and kissed him. Briefly. Fiercely. Passionately. This was time before time. Connected in the present, the past and the future. Tim brought me back down to earth. 'I've wanted to do that for a long time! From the day I pulled you onto the train.' He kissed me again and then let me go again. 'We do have to go.'

I sighed. 'I want to stay here in Sydney.'

'You'll be back on your birthday and then we can see each other before you return to Geelong.'

'Yes, I'll be back on 1st February. And then exams in June. After that, I'm coming back to Sydney.'

I kissed Tim again, and when we let go of each other, I declared: 'I don't want to go to Jakarta!'

'You promised your father you would, so you have to. It's your father, and you're going to celebrate Christmas with him. We'll see each other again soon,' said Tim. 'I don't intend to wait for another two years.' He kissed me and pulled me along behind him.

Hand-in-hand we walked slowly out of the Garden of Eden.

WHAT USE IS A FATHER LIKE THAT?

'There you are, then!' On Christmas eve, my father picked me up from the boat at Tandjong Priok, the port of Jakarta. He put his arms around me, 'There you are, then!' he repeated.

'Do you remember that you also said that two years ago when you picked me up in Singapore?'

My father shook his head. 'No, I don't remember that. I'm glad you're here.'

He seemed to be really happy to see me again and even gave me a hug. I didn't know what to make of that. He had never visited me in Geelong. I thought that he had brought me to Jakarta to show his girlfriend what a wonderful father he was. If I was so important to him, why hadn't he come to visit me at all?

'Did you have a good journey?'

'Yes, it was fine, although it was awfully long. First there was the flight, then fifteen hours by train to Brisbane, and then the boat.'

'There was no other way.'

'You could have come to Geelong.'

'Why would I have gone to Geelong? I want to be at home for Christmas.'

I wanted to say that I would have liked to have shown him my life there, and that it was safer in Australia than in Jakarta, where things were still messy. But if there was something that I had learnt at the Morongo Girls' College in Geelong, it was that it was best not to tell adults what you were thinking. That way, you avoided lots of clashes.

'Captain Somers sends his regards.'

'Did he look after you well?'

'He's a really nice man.'

We walked across the quay to his car. It was quite odd to be back in Java. The smell, in particular, was overwhelming. A curious mix of spices, diesel, flowers, coconut palms, fruit, fish and the sea. A smell that was so familiar. Only the Indies smelled like that. It was only now that I realized how different it was in Australia, and how I had missed these particular smells.

'I've rented a house in Menteng. I was fed-up with living in a hotel,' said my father, as he manoeuvred the car across the quay. 'It's a nice place in a lovely residential area.'

I had no idea what I was supposed to say and just stared out of the car window. I hadn't really found my father again. When we pulled up, Wendy was waiting for us in front of a white two-storey house. The house had a tiled roof, an open veranda and a front garden that was set back from the road by a low wall. I had never really met his girlfriend before. I had only caught a glimpse of her walking entwined with my father in Bondi, but I immediately recognised the woman with the thin shoulder-length bleached hair.

She greeted me with two kisses. 'Royal kisses,' my mother would have said: kisses accompanied by smacking noises directed into space. It always made my mother laugh if someone greeted her in that way, and I had the urge to titter now.

'Hello, Nell.'

I studied her face, which didn't seem to give much away. Thin lips, pale eyes and a chin that stuck out too far. My mother had been much more beautiful. I couldn't understand what my father saw in this woman.

'Hi…y-you're my father's girlfriend.' I eyed her challengingly. 'I'm his daughter.'

Wendy pursed her lips, looked at my father for a moment, and said: 'I'm Wendy, your father's wife.' She spoke a little sluggishly.

'Wife? Oh, you're getting married. Congratulations. When?'

'Well, actually it's like this… we're already married,' said my father.

'Already married? When?' I just couldn't believe what I was hearing, but I tried to stay calm.

'We were married in August,' answered Wendy.

'And I wasn't invited?'

'It was nothing, Nell,' shushed my father.

Wendy looked at him frostily. If looks could kill, my father would have dropped down dead instantly. 'What do you mean, it was nothing?'

My father sighed and smiled at Wendy. 'I only meant it was a small ceremony. That's all.'

I wouldn't be fobbed off. 'A ceremony that you didn't even invite me to!' I said.

'I'm sorry. Perhaps I should have done.'

'You write to me every week and you don't even tell me about something *that* important! How can you be like that? Even if you didn't want to invite me to the wedding, you could, at least, have told me. I'm your daughter!' I shouted that last bit. I was so angry. 'Perhaps for the sake of convenience you've forgotten about your daughter of almost eighteen, that you'd hidden away in a school in Australia for two years!'

Wendy took my travel bag and pushed me towards the house. 'Let's not stand around here. Come on, Nell, I'll show you to your room.'

I felt like shouting that she had to keep her hands off me but going inside with her was preferable to staying outside with my father and arguing.

In the guest room, the shutters were closed. It was dark and cool. Wendy put my bag on a small table next to the bed. 'You'll be tired from travelling. Have a rest and we'll see you later.' At the door, she stopped, as if she wanted to say something else, but then she walked out and shut the door softly behind her.

As soon as I was alone in the room, I sprawled on the bed. It was true, I was exhausted. I could have cried my eyes out, but I was afraid that once I started, I wouldn't be able to stop. So, I pulled myself together. I was annoyed that I had once again made the mistake of telling my father what I was thinking. I had hardly arrived, and we were already fighting again. *Stupid, stupid, stupid.*

I longed for Tim. Why hadn't I stayed with him in Sydney on the grass by the pond in the botanical gardens? The Tim I had got to know there, was different to the one who had visited me in Geelong. He was more like the boy I'd met on the train to Surabaya. Or was it me who had changed? I got up, took a sheet of airmail paper from my travel bag, and wrote Aunt Karly a letter.

GIRL OUT OF PLACE

Dear Auntie,

Tomorrow is Christmas. I'm at my father's house in Jakarta. Did you know he married Wendy, the woman who lent him the Ford? I think it's awful, and since I only just heard, that's even worse. But you being in Holland and me over here is the worst thing of all.

I wish I was with you for Christmas. Most of all, I wish I had stayed with Tim in Sydney. I met him there on my way here. I think I'm in love. But how do you know for sure? Do you remember our conversation about how you can reinvent yourself? Straight after, I made a list of what I knew about myself, and there were only things on it that other people had said about me. Luckily, the list looks quite different now:

1. I can't wait to turn 18, so that no-one can tell me what to do anymore. Especially my father.

2. I have a talent for the one thousand metres freestyle.

3. I've got a good strong body (from all the swimming, of course.)

4. I'm a good-looking young lady (thank you, mother).

5. I'm going to bury the war as deep as I can beneath new things.

6. I miss my mother more than my father.

7. I want to be with Tim to find out if we belong together. So, more kissing.

8. I often think about what I want to do with my life.

9. In the New Year, I hope to see my aunt as soon as possible in Australia.

So, I've changed a lot, but I'm still the same old Nell

too. Or has the old 'me' disappeared because of all the changes and the new experiences? Do you always turn into someone else, or is there a core to who you are, that you carry with you when you experience new things? I really don't know. I wish you a happy 1948, with me as part of it.

Love and hugs from afar,

Nell.

I closed my eyes and thought of Tim. And then I missed him more than ever. An absence that felt like physical pain with every beat of my heart. If only I had brought my mother's coat. That coat always comforted me.

'Are you enjoying yourself, Cornelia?' my father dared to ask, a week later. He was reading the paper in his armchair and, because I had nothing else to do, I was just sitting around with a book.

'Yes, it was a nice Christmas. A thousand times better than in Geelong.'

'Not too many guests?'

'No, guests are part of Christmas.' I meant it when I said that. I didn't say that I had hardly spoken to him, because he was hiding from me behind the visitors, and if he wasn't preoccupied with the guests, then Wendy was hanging on his arm, wobbling on her high heels.

'Good,' said my father, and he was about to hide behind his paper again, but now that I had him on his own for once, I wanted to discuss my return journey with him. I wanted to know when I would see Tim again.

'When do I go back to Sydney? How will I be travelling?'

Startled, he looked at me.

'Of course, today I'll celebrate New Year's Eve with you here, but I want to know when I'll be back in Australia. School starts on 2nd February and I'd like to meet friends in Sydney and then travel on to Geelong.'

'Well, here's the thing….' My father was searching for words.

'I can travel on my own. Somers doesn't have to pick me up and fly me to Geelong.'

'You're not going back to school, Cornelia,' sighed my father. 'It's too expensive. I can't pay for your tuition anymore.' His face seemed tight and frozen. The lines that ran down from his nose and pulled down the corners of his mouth gave him a surly expression that I knew all too well. That's the way he looked when it was hopeless trying to oppose him. That's the way he had looked when he first sent me to Geelong.

'They know you're not coming back.'

I felt the blood draining from my face. 'What do you mean? I have to go back to Geelong. They're expecting me! I'm sitting my final exams in a few months and I want to see my friends again.'

'I've discussed it with the school.'

I gasped for breath. I knew that if I started shouting, all would be lost. 'In any event, I want to go back to Australia. I won't go back to Geelong then and I'll stay in Sydney,' I said, as calmly as possible. I thought of Tim and the tears came forth unbidden.

'I've already booked the boat.'

'What boat?' This conversation was developing in completely the wrong direction and I couldn't do anything to turn the tide.

'I've booked a passage on the *Willem Ruys*. It's sailing for Holland on 2nd January.'

'I'm not going. I don't have a trunk that can be shipped.'

'Come on, don't make this harder than it already is,' said my father, as he nervously fingered the newspaper on his lap.

'Hard for me or for you? You're sending me away while you just stay here. If you hadn't got married, you could have afforded my school.'

'I've arranged a school for you that is affordable in the Netherlands. You can go to secondary school there.'

'I'm not going to school in Holland,' I shouted, now that I saw that all was lost. 'What am I supposed to do in Holland? Aunt Karly is the only person I know there. You sent me to Geelong. I was sixteen and I had no choice. You can't send me somewhere against my will again. I'm almost eighteen. You can't just do that!'

My father folded the paper, laid it on the table and got up.

'Almost eighteen is not yet eighteen. So, you'll do what I tell you.' Without looking at me he left the room.

I picked up the newspaper and tore it into shreds. Just like the newspaper, I had fallen apart into a thousand tiny pieces.

I didn't see my father for the rest of that day. It was the worst New Year's Eve ever. I stayed in my room. I shut out my feelings and started surviving day by day, just like I had survived the death of my mother and my exile to Geelong. I just couldn't believe what my father intended. No way was I going to pretend to be cheerful and celebrate New Year's Eve with him and Wendy. I hardly slept and dreamt that my father and Tim were playing pool together and they were completely ignoring me. I woke up crying. On New Year's Day, in the morning, I ran downstairs as soon as I heard my father getting up.

'Happy New Year, Nell. Cup of tea?' he asked when he saw me. He was pretending nothing had happened again and invitingly lifted the teapot.

'You can send me to the Netherlands, but I'm not going to school there!'

'You have to.'

'If I'm not allowed to go to Geelong, then I'm not going to school anymore. I'm too old for that.'

'Alright, no more school. Then you'll need to learn a trade, so that you can earn your own keep. You'll need to be independent at some point, Nell. I'll ask Aunt Karly to register you for a shorthand and typing course, and I'll send the money to Holland.'

I felt a chill run down my back. Auntie had known what was in store for me and hadn't warned me? It felt like a betrayal.

'So, you consult with Karly and not with me?' I asked angrily.

'There was no other way. She had to make some arrangements such as a place for you to live.'

'Am I going to live with Aunt Karly?' Unexpectedly, there was a ray of hope.

'No, she's found a place with Ida Stips, a cousin of mine. I don't know her, but Karly says that Ida has a spare room and that you are welcome there.'

'Please let me go to Australia,' I begged. But my father was unrelenting and stuck to his plan.

'I'm sorry, Cornelia. I'm only paying you an allowance if you get on that boat to the Netherlands. There is nothing more to be said.' He strode out of the dining room.

Dismayed, I watched him go. In my father's life, there only

seemed to be room for imperatives. Listen! Shut up! Leave! The boat had already been booked. Tomorrow, 2nd January, I would leave. It was all too familiar. It was exactly the same as when my father had sent me to Jakarta, to Bondi and to Geelong. But I wasn't going to let him dictate to me any longer. I wanted to take control of my own life. Once again, I had to reinvent myself.

I had just packed my travel bag when Wendy entered my room. I quickly covered my things with the bedspread.

Wendy set down a tray with a pot of jasmine tea, a porcelain teacup, and a small plate of biscuits on the mahogany dresser. 'I thought you might be thirsty.'

'You don't have to look after me.'

'I'm just trying to be nice to you while you're here.'

'That won't be for long, because thanks to you I'll be gone tomorrow. If you hadn't been here, my father would never have sent me to the Netherlands. If he hadn't married you, he wouldn't have taken me out of school.'

Wendy objected, but I wasn't listening. I couldn't stop the words from pouring out. 'If it wasn't for you, my father wouldn't have lured me to Jakarta with false promises, so he could put me on the boat. You'll be glad to be finally rid of me, so you have my father all to yourself. Well, you can have him, that father of mine. You can keep him. What's the use of a father who abandons his daughter for another woman?' I took two biscuits from the plate and crushed them in my hand.

Without saying anything, Wendy left the room.

I was still sitting on the edge of the bed. I felt awful. I had said everything I wanted to say, but it didn't change a thing.

I took a deep breath, brushed the crumbs off my hand, pulled my travel bag from beneath the bedspread and crept out of the house.

As soon as I was outside, I sprinted down the street. My heart thumped and it was only when I had turned the corner, that I breathed a sigh of relief, and walked on more calmly. I hardly knew the residential area where my father lived. Before the war, it must have been a lovely neighbourhood, with houses rendered in white, streets lined with trees, parks, gardens and squares. Now the plaster was hanging off the buildings, the gardens were badly kept, and everything seemed run-down. After a few streets, I came to the Oranje Nassau Boulevard. A little further on was the Nassau church, a big building with a tiled roof and a tall white steeple. The clock on the tower said it was two o'clock. Aimlessly, I continued on into town. With the last of my money, I sent a telegram to Tim in a post office. I only had enough money for six words:

'Father is sending me to Holland!'

I hoped he would understand my distress call. What an awful start to the new year. I walked on to the Koning's Square. I'd been there with my father during those two weeks that I had lived with him in Jakarta. I passed the palace of the Governor General, wandered around the old neighbourhood of Rijswijk and via a detour, arrived at Hotel des Indes. A tram was just passing. It would have been lovely to ride a tram through the city, but I didn't have any money.

I watched the tram go by and wandered on. To blend in, I kept walking. If I stopped, I didn't really feel comfortable. It seemed a long time since I had seen so many different people together out in the street: Indonesians, Malaysians, Arabs, Chinese, and Westerners. Here and there, I noticed groups of Dutch, British and British-Indian soldiers. For the last two years in Geelong, I had hardly seen any uniforms in the streets.

Their presence felt threatening. The war wasn't over yet in Jakarta. It gave me an awful fright when an army truck raced past me and screeched to a halt only ten metres ahead. That's how it was in Surabaya the day that Tim had been plucked from the street. In a panic, I fled into a park.

I sat on a bench as far away from the soldiers as I could get, until the shock had worn off. I reconsidered my options. Did I have a plan for the new life I would be inventing? Not really. Tomorrow, the *Willem Ruys* was leaving for Holland. I had to make sure my father didn't put me on that boat. After that, I'd just see what happened. But for the time being, I had to stay away from my father.

I roamed through the city and after a few hours, quite unexpectedly, I was standing in front of the Nassau church again. I had unintentionally walked a full circle and I couldn't go on, because it was almost dark. Lost in thought, I entered the porch of the church. The door wasn't locked. I stepped into the church, and for a while I just sat on a bench in the back of the sparsely lit room. It was dark outside now. *Should I go home? No! Impossible!* I could envisage smoke coming from my father's ears if I got home that late. And then tomorrow morning, he would deliver me straight to the port. He would never relent. No! I had no choice but to stay here! The church was a fine shelter for the night. No-one would look for me here. I only had to stay awake and be off tomorrow before people came to church.

I couldn't last a whole evening sitting on a wooden bench. After two hours, I crept under a pew and put my head on my travel bag. *Don't sleep. Stay awake.* Tomorrow, I had to be off before anyone came to church. How would I ever get back to Sydney? Had Tim received my telegram? Would he understand? Silence descended. My mother woke me and whispered: 'Come with me. You're not safe here. You're better off sleeping with me in the field. I won't be so lonely then.

Come.' She put a hand on my shoulder. The hand was cold and heavy. I tried to shake it off, but I couldn't. 'I'm not coming!' I shouted.

'It's alright,' spoke a low voice. The hand let go. 'It's alright.' I opened my eyes and looked around me, confused. *How stupid! I had fallen asleep. Stupid, stupid, stupid!* A man was squatting next to me. It had to be the vicar, with that black suit and a white collar around his neck.

'I don't want to scare you, but the floor of the church is not the best place to sleep. You'd better come with me to the vicarage.' He stood up, put out his hand and pulled me out from under the pew. Quickly, I looked around me. Was there an escape route?

'Why does a young lady like you need a place to sleep in my church?' The vicar guided me along the aisle to the other side of the church where a door gave access to the vicarage. He pushed open the door. 'Welcome to my inn.' The door closed behind me. There was no way out. The vicar sat me down at the table in the big kitchen of the vicarage. Then he rummaged around in the pantry and placed a bowl of rice and spicy green beans and a glass of water in front of me. 'I'm sure you're hungry.' He looked on in a friendly way as I shamelessly gulped down the food.

When I had emptied the bowl and pushed it away, he looked at me inquiringly. 'Haven't we met before? Aren't you Arends' daughter?'

'I'm not from around here. I don't know you.' I felt my face turning red. I hoped he wouldn't notice.

'I have seen you before, but we didn't talk when I was over at your father's and mother's place on Christmas day.'

I blushed even more. 'Stepmother.'

'Stepmother, and you must be?'

'Nell Arends. I'm sorry. I don't know why I didn't say that straight away.'

'I'm sure you have your reasons. I'd like to listen to your story, but first I'm going to call a messenger boy, to take a note to your father that you're here. He must be worried.' The vicar got up and left me alone in the kitchen.

I put my head on my arms. Tears of frustration ran down my face. I could predict exactly how this would end. Everything was lost now. After just half a day, the mission to reinvent myself had come to nothing in this church.

At nine o'clock in the morning, my father and Wendy took me by car to Tandjong Priok. I saw the *Willem Ruys* lying moored at the quay. I couldn't bear to look at the ship and closed my eyes. Since my father had picked me up at the Nassau church the night before, we hadn't spoken a word. The vicar tried to discuss my departure with my father, but to no avail. He shouldn't have notified him. I could have told him that straight off.

In silence, my father had walked me to my room and had locked the door behind me. My own father had robbed me of my freedom and there was nothing I could do. I just had to accept that he was the one in charge.

This morning, he had made me get into the car. I was sitting in the back of the car with my blue, checked travel bag on my lap. The sound of the car door opening made me look up, and I got out slowly. Wendy gave me two 'royal kisses', and I just let them wash over me. With both arms, my father held me tightly for a moment. 'Safe journey, Cornelia.'

I broke free. I couldn't bear him touching me. 'I know I have to do what you say for now. You can send me to Holland because I'm not yet eighteen. But in a month, I will be, and then I can go back to Australia. And that's what I'm going to do. I'm not going to let you run my life anymore.'

'You're angry at me now. When some time has passed, you'll think differently. Then you'll say that your father did the right thing for you.'

'I don't think so. Why would I be less angry in a while? You'll still be exactly the same and carry on pretending there's nothing wrong.'

'We'll wait to see you off. Goodbye, Cornelia.'

In silence, I walked up the gangway to the *Willem Ruys*. I didn't look back.

After some searching, I found my cabin. It was a cabin for two people, but only one bed was made. I was lucky, I was the only passenger. In the cabin, I saw a small familiar trunk. It was my father's trunk, that he had had with him on our trip to America. I dropped down on top of the trunk and began to sob loudly. The ship's horn sounded twice. It marked our departure to a country where I had never been, and where the only person I knew was my Aunt Karly. Auntie, who had also betrayed me.

I wasn't going to go on deck, but then I changed my mind. I wasn't going to let myself be dictated to by my father. This might be the last time I would ever see the coastline of Java. I slammed the door of my cabin behind me and ran to the upper deck. Slowly, the ship started moving.

I looked at the quay and saw my father. I didn't wave. I would stay there until Java had slowly dissolved into thin air and the horizon consisted only of the sea.

WHERE'S THE SUN?

When I arrived on the *Willem Ruys* in Rotterdam from Jakarta in late January, I had spent the whole journey having imaginary arguments with Auntie about how she had betrayed me, because she had helped my father to put me on the boat to Holland. Aunt Karly came to pick me up and as soon as I came down the gangway, she ran to me in the rain, took me in her arms and rocked me back and forth. It felt like coming home – familiar and safe. My anger disappeared. I knew immediately that Aunt Karly had never deserted me.

'I'm so glad to see you, dear Nell. It's been such a long time!' she said.

'Too long, Auntie, much too long,' I answered.

'I tried to stop those wretched plans of your father. He could have got married later. He should have let you finish school. But he had already thought it all out and told me his plan on the telephone.'

'I ran away the day before the boat left but the vicar took me home. He told my father it would be better if I could finish school in Australia. Of course, my father didn't listen and now I'm here.'

'Don't think that I agreed with him.'

'Of course not!'

'But you did think that. I know you, Nell! Believe me, however glad I am to have you here with me, I disagreed with your father from the beginning!'

There was no-one who knew me as well as Auntie. I tried to reassure her. 'I know. There's no stopping my father. Now I'm here, and we're together again, we've got ourselves soaking wet out here on the quay!'

Then Aunt Karly and I travelled by train to The Hague, to Cousin Ida Stip's house, where I was given a tiny, freezing-cold room. 'Dear Nell, you need some sleep and some time to get used to your new surroundings. I'll see you tomorrow', said my aunt, and off she went.

On the bed, there was a large package containing my mother's coat and a letter!

I would like to be with you, Nell, but I can't afford the trip at the moment. After I got your telegram, I travelled to Geelong and heard that your father had taken you out of school. What a mess. I took your personal possessions that you'd left at school with me, including your mother's coat. They wanted to send your stuff to your father in Jakarta, but I know how important that coat is for you and how much comfort it brings you. And because they know me there, they let me have everything. I won't have saved up enough for the passage until the end of July. That's why I'm sending the coat on ahead by airmail. I'll come as soon as I can!

XX

Tim.'

Such a lovely letter!

I read that letter again and again until I knew the words by heart. That first night in Holland, I slept in my mother's coat. I dreamt that we were walking on the deck of the *Willem Ruys* together in the coat, like Siamese twins, each with one arm up the sleeve of the coat and the other wrapped around each other. Tim was right. I would never have survived here without my mother's coat. I was always cold and missed Tim more than I could bear.

Just as she'd promised, Aunt Karly came to see me the day after my arrival. It was my birthday, but I didn't feel like doing anything.

'From now on, we're going to meet every Sunday at Hotel des Indes at the Lange Voorhout. Starting from today,' she said.

Before I could object, Auntie said firmly: 'And I won't accept no for an answer. So, put on your coat.'

'To do what?' I felt displaced and didn't feel like going anywhere.

'We're going to celebrate your eighteenth birthday and Hotel des Indes is the perfect place for that.'

I hadn't quite conceded yet. 'Why should we go there?'

'Because Hotel des Indes has a certain type of elegance that cheers a person up. That's why it's a good place to meet up regularly.'

'There's a Hotel des Indes in Jakarta, too.'

'Yes, I went there often with my Chris.'

'I was there with my father once, and on New Year's Day, I walked past it.'

'In The Hague, Hotel des Indes looks very different, but I like going there because it still reminds me of the Indies. If we meet there every Sunday, I'm sure you won't waste away from homesickness in this dump. Come on, get your coat and let's go.'

From that afternoon on, I had tea with Aunt Karly every Sunday in the most beautiful spot in The Hague. And it's a good thing I did. Our Sunday afternoon tea was my lifeline.

I was looking forward to our meeting one Sunday in April. It was raining just as hard as when I had arrived in Rotterdam from Jakarta. I had to hurry. I would regret every minute that I missed of her company, so I absolutely did not want to be late. I should have left earlier, but the rain delayed everything. The sky was threateningly grey, almost black, and there was a strong wind blowing. It was always windy in The Hague, but that day the wind had a real chill, and because of the rain, it was awful outside. The long, continuous downpour reminded me of the warm monsoon rains in the Indies. Just for a moment, I could feel the rain of the Indies and smell the wet earth until the cold rain of The Hague swept it all away. For a moment, I could almost touch the past. I shivered and quickened my pace.

I longed for the Spring, the sun, and blue skies. Apparently, there was such a thing in Holland, but I hadn't experienced it yet. By the time I got to the Hotel des Indes, I was like a half-drowned rat and when I handed in my dripping wet coat at the cloakroom, the staff greeted me warmly. By now, they knew me as a regular Sunday afternoon customer. I was on time, which was the main thing. My feet sank into the beautiful red Persian rug that covered the floor of the restaurant. I passed through the marble columns that supported the high ceiling and beyond the panelling with gold trim until I reached our usual spot close to the big palm in the white pot, which seemed to brandish its wide leaves at the guests. I saw immediately that

Aunt Karly hadn't arrived yet. Although I was shivering as I waited, I could feel myself thawing a little bit as it was nice and warm inside the restaurant.

I curled up in the plush red velvet chair and waited for my aunt. She'd be here soon. I couldn't imagine my cousin Ida ever coming here. Strange that I was thinking of her now. I hadn't seen her since I'd moved out of her house to rent my little attic by the sea. I was so glad that I wasn't living-in with her anymore, and that I wasn't going to those stupid typing lessons that my father had arranged for me. I had really tried. I had done exactly what was required of me, attending those lessons every day despite it making me so unhappy. Then all of a sudden Aunt Karly was standing beside me. I hadn't heard her approaching on the Persian rug.

'A penny for your thoughts, Nell!' She kissed me. She looked lovely with her shoulder-length hair held back by a purple silk headscarf, which coloured her blue eyes violet.

'Just one thought,' I answered happily. 'I have a beautiful aunt!' I kissed Aunt Karly and held out my hand. 'That's a penny then.'

Aunt Karly laughed. 'By the sound of it, you're doing fine, Nell.'

The waiter brought over a tray with a china teapot, a tea-strainer on a small saucer, two teaspoons, two china cups, a small jug of milk, a pot of sugar, a silver bowl of chocolates and some cinnamon cake, and he moved everything skilfully from the tray to the table. We ordered the same thing every Sunday, so they brought it to us automatically.

'I mean it,' she said, when we had poured our tea. 'You're looking really well!'

'It's so nice to be eighteen, to make my own decisions and not be answerable to anyone else! It's wonderful!' I said, with my mouth full of cinnamon cake. 'I think I'll stay eighteen for the rest of my life.'

'If only that were possible.'

'That first Sunday we were here in Hotel des Indes, do you remember…?'

Auntie nodded.

'We sat here at this very same table and then you gave me the most beautiful birthday present I have ever had: that small portrait of me and my mother. She had it painted in the Ambarawa camp by a woman in exchange for food or something. My mother looks serious in it and I'm standing to the right of her, but I don't have a face. It hasn't been filled in.'

'That's because Elenore died. It was never finished.'

'I know, but when I looked at the portrait that evening in my room, I thought: "I'm like the girl in that painting, a bit of a blank space." It's time that girl got a face. My father knows exactly what that girl should look like, what she should become. You have ideas about that, too, but I have to shape her for myself. My life has been completely mapped out by others. Especially by my father! I need to shape my own life. You told me that in Bondi once, do you remember?'

'Yes, because I thought you needed to think about that, but you were just sixteen, Nell! It's not so easy at that age.'

'I did try, though. But it wasn't until I got here, that I realized that my life took a turn of its own, after you left Bondi. I was seeing Nathan, but whenever we kissed, I found myself thinking of Tim. On my birthday that summer, Nathan suddenly appeared at the beach with Tim. It was so confusing, seeing those two boys together like that. And the next day I was packed off to Geelong by my father. Two years later, I was barely back on track when, completely unexpectedly, I fell in love with Tim. At least, I think I'm in love with him. Then suddenly, my father sent me over here and when I arrived, I felt terribly lost for a while. But now it's different.'

Aunt Karly poured the tea again. 'No shorthand and typing for you anymore?'

'No! My father can go take a running jump. I prefer working at the American Embassy like I'm doing now.'

'How nice to be independent, thanks to that job.'

'Yes, I earn enough to live on, and the work is fun. Just last week, I gave a group of American doctors a tour of The Hague and I'm organising an international conference in May in the Kurhaus in Scheveningen.'

'Have you heard anything from Tim yet?'

'No, I only know he's coming at the end of July.' I immediately felt my whole body tensing as I said that. That was three whole months away. I might have fallen out of love by then.

'It will soon pass,' she reassured me, as if she had read my thoughts. 'At least you've got a nice place of your own now. It's a good thing that you found that room through your work and moved out of Ida's place.'

'Yes, I'm really happy with my room by the sea.' I put the last piece of cake into my mouth and then I had another chocolate. 'I can see the sand dunes from the loft window. If the wind is coming from the right direction, I can hear the sea just like in Bondi. I've got the whole loft to myself. I can do whatever I want. The lady who is renting it out, hardly bothers with me at all. It's wonderful!' I sipped my tea. 'And you, Auntie, how are things at your in-laws?'

'It doesn't look like my mother-in-law is going to recover, so she needs me to take care of her. She's pleased to have me there because we can grieve for her son Chris together. I don't know what the future will bring, or whether I'll even stay here in Holland.'

'I can't do without you, Aunt Karly! We've only just got back together again.'

'We'll always find each other, Nell. I don't know where life will take me. I'm missing the Indies. The way it was before the war.'

'Me too, sometimes. Would you like to go back to the Indies?'

'Yes, I'd love to go back if there was a future for me there, but I don't think things are going to work out like that. It's just a matter of time, before the Indonesians throw out anyone they think doesn't fit in with the new Republic.'

'My father, too? I actually quite like it that he's so far away he can't meddle in my life anymore.'

'You'd better be off before he gets here, then,' said Aunt Karly, laughing. 'Do you answer his letters?'

I shook my head no. 'Maybe, someday.'

'Shall we have another pot of tea?'

'Lovely. More cake?'

'Absolutely,' said Aunt Karly. 'I'm in no hurry on Sundays. It's much too cosy here with you.'

And that's how it went every week. I lived from Sunday to Sunday. I never arranged to meet anyone on that day. Sundays were just for Aunt Karly and me. Until the doorbell rang on the second Sunday of May.

I'M HERE FOR YOU

'Tim? How–? That's impossible! It's only the 16th of May today. I thought you weren't coming for another two months!'

'Hello, dear Nell. Should I come back again later?' teased Tim, as he hugged me.

'No, of course not!' I crept into his arms and we kissed. It felt familiar and awkward at the same time.

'I'm not letting you send me away, anyway,' said Tim. 'I'm really pleased I got the chance to see you now. I wanted to surprise you. My work made some arrangements and then I could fly for free, so I packed my bags immediately.'

'It's certainly a surprise! Have you flown before?'

'No, not everyone has a father who is a pilot! It was the first time. I thought it was brilliant!'

'And flying is incredibly fast! I'm so glad you're here!' I wriggled free from his arms. 'Let me just get my bag and then we can go to the beach.'

Half an hour later, we were walking together in Scheveningen beside the sea. It was Sunday and there were a lot of people out enjoying the beautiful weather.

'Do you smell Spring in the air?'

Tim shrugged his shoulders. 'Not really.'

'Doesn't matter. Perhaps you need to be here longer to be able to smell it, but it's definitely there. I could jump for joy, that we're walking here together. At last.'

'It's as if I saw you only yesterday in Sydney. You've just never been away.'

'This beach is my favourite place. I come here often. My loft is small, but here I have all the space in the world.'

'I can imagine you wanting to be here, but I'm surprised it's so busy! It's absolutely freezing!' Tim pulled his winter coat more tightly around him.

'You're not used to this climate. It was the same for me when I arrived at the end of January. And you're so lucky, Tim! By Dutch standards, this is a warm day in May. When I arrived late January, the temperature was just above zero, but you get used to it. I'm the living proof of that.'

Tim bent down at the water's edge and scooped up some seawater with his hand. He shivered. 'The water's freezing cold.' He dried his hand on his coat and put an arm around my shoulder. Side by side, we walked on along the shore. The rough material of his coat tickled my neck, but I didn't care. Tim pulled me closer to him and kissed me. His lips tasted salty. A big wave came rushing in just then forcing us apart. We only just avoided being soaked.

'Do you remember in Sydney, that I told you, that your father keeps sending you away every time I catch up with you? In Bondi, in Sydney! I just couldn't believe it that he wouldn't let you go back to Geelong and sent you here, instead.'

'He can't send me anywhere anymore. I'm looking after myself now. I've got a job, a place to live and I'm saving up.

When I've got enough money, I'm going back to Sydney. Then I can swim in the sea again!'

'Do you hear anything from your father?'

'He writes to me regularly, but his letters don't mean anything. I haven't answered them. I prefer writing letters to you.'

Silently, I walked with Tim from the sea up into the sand dunes where we dropped down onto the sand. 'What is the height of patience?' I asked Tim.

'Well?'

'Falling in love with you and waiting for you to finally turn up!'

Tim laughed, grabbed hold of me and together we rolled like little children over the sand and down the side of the dune. We lay there for a while, stretched out side by side. Then I got up and brushed the sand off my dress.

'Come on. We're going to Hotel des Indes, to meet Aunt Karly. Every Sunday, I have tea there with her, and I've never missed once.'

Tim was staying at a small hotel in Scheveningen not far from my loft. On Monday, after I had finished work, he came to The Hague and together we strolled through the city. It was still beautiful weather and we walked hand-in-hand from the Malieveld, past the Binnenhof to Noordeinde Palace.

'I never knew there were so many benches in The Hague,' I remarked with surprise.

'Maybe you never sit on them?'

'I do, but I didn't know how nice it was to sit on them with your boyfriend.'

'And it's even nicer when your boyfriend kisses you while you're sitting on the bench!'

'I had no idea how nice that could be.' I dragged Tim to the next bench, excitedly. I had taken the rest of the week off work. On Wednesday, we went for a bike ride through the dunes together.

'It's beautiful here with all the different colours of the grass. I could live here.'

'I thought you found it too cold here.'

'I could live here with the heating on.'

'Cycling fast also helps! Race you to Katwijk!' I cried, and immediately pedalled off.

Before long, Tim was riding beside me. 'Bet I'm there first!'

Both red in the face, we arrived together at the beach access. 'It's a draw,' I cried.

'It was a false start,' joked Tim, 'so I won.'

We threw the bikes down against the sand dune and raced to the beach.

'I won!' and with an advantage of ten metres, Tim dropped down in the sand by a beach post.

'Fine by me.' I dropped down beside him. We sat close together and looked at the sea. I felt connected with everything around me. I thought of my mother. I was sure she would have liked Tim.

'Look at those little birds running so fast with their tiny legs across the sand!'

'They're little stints. They run and fly up above the surf, just as they're about to get their feet wet.'

'They're funny.' Tim came and knelt in the sand in front of me. 'You're funny, too, Nell. From the first day I saw you on the train to Surabaya. From that first look of yours, you had me, and I wanted to be with you.'

I laughed, then I took Tim's face in my hands, and looked into his eyes.

'I've spent a damn long time looking for you too. You make me laugh with your bad jokes.' I crept onto his lap, wrapped my legs around his waist and we sat like that for a long time on the beach.

'I still can't believe you're here.'

'Me neither.'

'It feels perfectly natural to be here with you on a sunny Friday in May in this restaurant in Scheveningen.' I looked at Tim, affectionately. He lifted his glass and made a toast chinking mine: 'To us!'

'To us!' I took a sip and put my glass down. 'How long are you staying?'

Tim shrugged. 'I don't know. Well…no… that's not strictly true, Nell.' Tim sighed and took my hands.

I tried to stay serious, but the solemnity with which Tim said my name made me laugh.

'No, really. I have to tell you something. I've been offered a job by a big advertising company in New York.'

I swallowed to hide my sudden fear. 'Fantastic. You must be good at what you do, then.' Nervously, I tapped the ground with my foot. Did I want to have this conversation?

'The company is paying for my trip to America and has arranged an apartment for me there. I'm just passing through Holland. I'll be taking the Holland-America line to New York shortly.'

'Why didn't you tell me this before?' I asked, stunned.

'I don't know. I wanted to, but there was never a good moment. I wanted to tell you, but I…well, I just didn't get round to it.'

'But you can't keep something like that to yourself for so long!'

'You're right, Nell, it's stupid, I know, but I was hoping that you might come with me to America.' Expectantly, Tim looked at me. 'What do you think?'

I didn't answer immediately. My mind was in turmoil and it felt as if my head was about to explode. Of course, I wanted to go with him. But he had sprung his plans for America on me so suddenly. What was I going to do there? I would have preferred to go back to Australia with Tim, to pick up from the moment where we had left off. I wanted to lie with him on the grass in the Royal Botanic Gardens and look at the Nell-and-Me-Pine tree. I wanted to restart my life at the point where my father had sent it off in a different direction. 'When do you leave?'

'Sunday.'

'Sunday! And you're only telling me now!'

Tim put both his hands up in the air and let them drop again. 'I'm sorry. I'm really sorry. I should have told you earlier, but I couldn't. It would have spoilt everything this week. Wouldn't it?'

I stayed silent. I was fuming.

'You could come a month later, Nell. I know that you can't just run off and leave things here. Just as long as you come!'

I nodded and pushed my plate aside. I didn't feel like eating anymore.

❈

I slept badly that night. I hadn't dreamt about my mother for a few months. Probably because I felt I had to get on with my life, and so I tried not to think about her so often. Now I had a familiar dream again. I was standing with my mother by the Surf Life Saving Club in Bondi. 'Take care, Nelly,' said my mother. 'Appearances can be deceiving.' I woke up in a sweat. I had to talk to Tim! Outside, it was drizzling, but I didn't take any notice. It was impossible to stay in my loft with all those thoughts running through my mind. I went for a long walk through the dunes and then I took a tram to The Hague, where I had arranged to meet Tim in a little place at the Spui. He was already sitting at a table when I went in, bedraggled from the rain.

'I'm not ready,' I said, even before I had taken off my wet coat. 'I don't know if I want to go to America. Don't you want to go back to Bondi with me? I've been saving up for that for a few months now, to go back to Australia.'

'Do you want to go back because of Nathan?' asked Tim, tensely.

'No! Whatever makes you think that?'

'You were seeing him, weren't you? When you were on the swimming team together?'

'Yes and no. I liked him, and I didn't know if I would ever see you again. He went to university and I never heard from him again. And that's not what this is about. I belong with you and not with Nathan. But what's going on with you? If I really mean something to you, why didn't you tell me straight away that you were only stopping off here on your way to America?'

'I love you. You know that.'

'Yes, perhaps that's true, but that's not enough.'

'I really love you. Come on, say you'll come with me!' begged Tim.

I felt pressurised, light-headed, as if I had been swimming too fast. I wished I could go with Tim, but my whole being was protesting against it. I was eighteen and had just started my own life. I wasn't going to be sent anywhere anymore. Tim wasn't my father! He might not be sending me to America, but he wasn't leaving me much choice, either. Could I say no and let him go alone, come what may? No, he would just have to stay here with me.

'What do you think? Will you come?' asked Tim.

'If you want to drag me to the other side of the world, then take me to Australia. I can't give up everything for you.'

Tim sat with his elbows on the table, his head resting in his hands. He looked very pale.

'I can't, Nell. I've already accepted that job.'

I pushed my chair back as the tears began to run down my cheeks. 'I can't go to America with you. I'm sorry.'

Tim swallowed hard and put his hand on top of mine. 'Then I'll wait for you.'

I laughed through my tears. 'So, you're staying here?'

'I'll wait for you over there. I hope you'll come to America one day soon.'

I stayed silent. I felt like knocking everything off the table with one sweep of my hand.

'I'll be back in a year: 21st May 1949. Let's meet here.'

'Maybe.'

'Same place, same time. Promise?'

I took a deep breath and said: 'Promise.'

A NEW DESTINATION

'You can still turn back,' said Aunt Karly, as we stood on the quay in Rotterdam, saying goodbye to each other.

I smiled. Only Auntie could say that. She knew me so well. When Tim left for New York a year ago, I'd felt just as lost as when I'd first arrived in Holland. That first Sunday afternoon after his departure, I had drunk tea just as usual with Auntie in Hotel des Indes at the Lange Voorhout.

'He just ran out on me,' I complained. I was furious with Tim. 'He shouldn't have done that, or else he shouldn't have come to The Hague at all.'

Aunt Karly didn't indulge me in my self-pity.

'It was your choice to stay here,' she said. 'That was a good decision, but now you have to make this work, otherwise you might as well have gone with him.'

'That's the stupidest thing I've ever heard. What nonsense,' I said, but of course Aunt Karly was right. Obviously, I regretted not having gone to America, but later on, I'd got used to the idea that Tim was over there, and that I was in The Hague. He could never have stayed with me here, anyway. Now he was in America instead of Australia. I had already waited for him for so long, that I decided I could endure another year. I'd just wait for him to come back in May. I wrote to him often. At first, Tim wrote back, but then his letters had stopped coming so regularly.

21st May came around the next year and I went back to the little café at the Spui as arranged. I couldn't wait to see him again.

'Same place, same time,' Tim had promised, but he wasn't there. I couldn't believe that he hadn't turned up, so I waited and waited until just before closing time. Then I cycled home, and I couldn't stop crying. I felt like my heart was breaking. For about a month the feeling of being lost and alone weighed on me until I decided that it was time to go back to Bondi.

'If you want to find out what the situation between you and Tim is, you must go and visit him and not go to Australia,' Aunt Karly advised.

'That's true,' I said, 'but I already know the answer. He wasn't at the Spui and that says it all.'

Aunt Karly didn't really agree with that. Even here on the quay she made a last attempt to get me to change my mind.

'That boat will leave for Melbourne anyway, with or without you.'

'No, it's fine the way it is. Tim isn't coming back, so I don't have to wait for him anymore. And I'm really looking forward to being in Bondi again. So, I'll see you there. I hope you'll visit really soon!'

'Of course! I can't do without you, Nell. I'm going to stay with my mother-in-law a little while longer, and then I'll come out to Australia. That won't be long. Write to me often and if something's the matter, call me.'

We hugged each other tight for a moment. 'Bye, Nell!'

'Goodbye, dear Auntie.'

From the upper deck, I waved goodbye to her. The ship's horn signalled our departure. A lot had happened since I had arrived in the harbour of Rotterdam a year and a half ago. It had rained cats and dogs then, but now the sun was shining and there was a light summer breeze. I didn't stay on the upper deck for long. It was too hard, having to leave Aunt Karly behind in The Hague. Lost in thought, I went inside and instantly crashed into someone, who had appeared out of thin air.

It was Tim! 'Hello, Nell.'

On hearing his voice, I felt my whole body go hot and cold. 'I can't believe bumping into you here like this! You're too late, Tim Thissen! We were supposed to meet in The Hague on 21st of May. That's two months ago.'

'I know. I'm sorry, Nell.'

'You weren't there. I sat there for hours, waiting for you.'

'I'm really sorry.'

'What are you doing here? Shouldn't you be in America?' I needled him.

'Where are you going?' he asked, pulling me towards him.

'Bondi, where else?' I pushed him away. 'This boat is going to Melbourne and then I'm travelling on to Sydney. Why did you hardly write to me for the past few months?'

Tim looked at me uncertainly and shrugged.

'And why are you on this boat, anyway?' I asked crossly.

'To ask you to forgive me if you can. I had a really big assignment which kept me way too busy and then when I realized how much I missed you, I came straight back to Rotterdam.'

I stared at him intensely but felt myself softening at his words.

'I should have let you know. By the time I arrived here, it was too late. Luckily, I heard that you were going to board this ship today.'

'Let me guess. You spoke to Aunt Karly?'

'Who else?'

I shook my head in disbelief.

'Come on, let's wave goodbye to her together. Maybe we'll still catch a glimpse of her.' Tim took my hand and pulled me back in the direction of the door to the upper deck.

The people on the quay had become so small that Aunt Karly was almost indiscernible on the quayside.

Tim leant against the railing. 'It was foolish of me to be so late. Please forgive me.' He laughed and looked like the boy I had fallen in love with again.

'That's not funny.'

He grabbed my hands. 'Nell, will you marry me?'

'Marry you?' The ship felt like it was spinning around me. I was caught completely off-guard.

'I know I've no right to ask you, but I want you to be my wife. That's why I came back.'

I was silent and looked at Tim.

'Please, say yes. I wanted to ask you a long time ago.'

'So why didn't you?'

'You were so angry that I was going to America that I didn't dare ask you. I thought you would say no.' Tim removed a black cord from around his neck. It was the cord with his father's ring that I had given him in Bondi. He untied the ring and slipped it on my finger.

'Please, say yes,' he said again.

I looked at the ring on my finger and put my hand on Tim's mouth to stop him saying anything else. Then I took my hand away and kissed his lips.

'So that's a yes?' asked Tim, timidly.

'Yes. Maybe…I don't know. I've got a job in Sydney with an airline. First, I want to learn to fly. I'm going to be a pilot.' I kissed him again.

'Where will you fly to first when you've got your license?'

'To Semarang. I want to fly a victory lap over my mother's grave at the Kalibanteng memorial cemetery.

'Can I come, too?'

'Of course!'

'So, you'll marry me?'

'Maybe. I really don't know.' Again, I looked at the ring on my finger. 'If I knew for sure that we belong together, I'd marry you straight away. But how can you be sure?'

'I'm totally sure about it. I think you will be, too, when we spend some more time together,' said Tim.

'And America? What about America?'

'Without you, there's nothing for me in America! I can work for advertising companies anywhere.'

I put my arms around him, and we kissed again. We kissed for a long time, as the seagulls screamed and soared overhead, and the S.S. *Volendam* steamed her way along the Nieuwe Waterweg towards the North Sea.

Glossary

Anjing Belanda – 'dogs of the Dutch' (derogatory term referring to people of mixed Indonesian-European descent)

Belanda – Dutchman

Belanda tabe – bye bye Dutchman

Bersiap – Literally: Be prepared. Refers to the chaotic months following WWII, when Indonesian freedom fighters fought for independence

Bungkusan – bundle of clothes

Gedek – bamboo fencing

Glatiks – paddy birds

Merdeka – freedom

Nasi – fried rice

Pasar – market

Pemuda – Indonesian freedom fighter

Pisang – banana

Tjemara – Indonesian fir tree

Author's End Note

Seven years ago, I became friends with Nora Valk. She inspired me to write *Girl Out Of Place*. This book is an adaptation of her life story, but it is still, of course, fiction.

I came to know Nora as an incredibly inquisitive and lively woman. It was only later that I learnt more about her life. Nora was born in 1930 in the Dutch East Indies. Her mother was English, and her father, who had also been born in the Indies, was a pilot in the Netherlands East Indies Army (KNIL). Nora had a carefree childhood. In 1940, she travelled with her father and mother to America, where Nora's father tested airplanes that the KNIL was thinking of buying.

After a year, the family returned to Java and six months later, in January 1942, the Japanese attacked the Dutch East Indies. On 28th February 1942, Japanese troops landed on Java. Military personnel, among them Nora's father, were taken away by the Japanese as prisoners of war. Nora and her mother were interned in an enclosed area in Surabaya, in a house with five or six other families. A few months later they were transferred to the Ambarawa camp in the middle of Java.

After the capitulation of Japan on 15th August 1945, Nora went looking for her father, whom she hadn't seen since the internment. Her mother died in the Ambarawa camp three months before Japan capitulated.

I wondered how much resilience and spirit one needed to go through all that, and then still develop into such a complete person as Nora. I became curious about the girl she used to be.

Seventy-five years after the war in the Dutch East Indies ended, I hope this book will find its way to the reader, so that this history is passed on. So that we will never forget.

Above: On board the ship bound for Singapore
Below: Nora Valk aged 15, taken in Bondi

Above: Nora Valk aged 16 in school uniform
Below: The M.S. *Willem Ruys* c 1948

If you liked this you might like:
The Colour of Things Unseen
by Annee Lawrence
9781912430178

The River's Song
by Suchen Christine Lim
9781906582982

Shambala Junction
by Dipika Mukherjee
9871910798393

Pomegranate Sky
by Louise Soraya Black
9871906582104

Kipling and Trix
by Mary Hamer
9781906582340

The Evolutionist
Avi Sirlin
9781906582531

**For more great books go to
www.aurorametro.com**